Recurring Fictions

Recurring

Fictions

 The University of
Alberta Press

Wendy McGrath

Published by
The University of Alberta Press
Ring House 2
Edmonton, Alberta T6G 2E1

NATIONAL LIBRARY OF CANADA CATALOGUING IN
PUBLICATION DATA

McGrath, Wendy.
    Recurring fictions

    ISBN 0–88864–389–6

    I. Title.
PS8575.G74R42 2002   C813'.6   C2002–910293–6
PR9199.3.M3172R42 2002

A volume in (cuRRents), a Canadian literature series. Jonathan Hart, series editor.
Printed and bound in Canada by Houghton-Boston, Saskatoon, Saskatchewan.
∞ Printed on acid-free paper.
Proofreading by Tara Taylor and Alethea H. Adair.

The University of Alberta Press is committed to protecting our natural environment.
As part of our efforts, this book is printed on stock produced by New Leaf Paper: it
contains 100% post-consumer recycled fibres and is acid- and chlorine-free.

The University of Alberta Press acknowledges the financial support of the
Government of Canada through the Book Publishing Industry Development Program
for its publishing activities. The Press also gratefully acknowledges the support
received for its program from the Canada Council for the Arts.

The Canada Council | Le Conseil des Arts
FOR THE ARTS | DU CANADA
SINCE 1957 | DEPUIS 1957

Canadä

For John

There is the house we all inhabit

the house which is the body and only the body

Where ghostly families in the corridors of the blood

record their odd abbreviated histories

—GWENDOLYN MACEWEN, "The Yellow House"

one

Johnny Cash played the
harmonica imitating the sound of trains. You couldn't see
the harmonica it was covered by his hands   his hands
closed over the harmonica moving back and forth over his
mouth. It seemed his mouth made the sound not the
harmonica not a train but   his mouth   his mouth became
that harmonica his mouth became the sound of the train.

His mouth blew in and out of the square holes   just
the rhythm the rhythm of the train and the shapes inside
the harmonica were the shapes of the tracks and the man
in black blew air in and out   breathing in the sound of
trains every train that ever travelled.

Inmates clapped

　　　　　　clapped for the man in black

　　　　　　　　　　clapped for the sound

of trains. He made the sound　　live at Folsom Prison. And

those men clapped and for a few short seconds they were on

those trains and they were whistling like those trains long

sad train whistles lost in the shapes inside the tracks in the

shapes inside the harmonica. Their mouths drawn tight

over fingers whistling　　the sound of trains　　whistling the

shape of the tracks

　　　　　　whistling.

The note of a song she could never allow herself to sing.

Dream:

I lie in bed in a public place and bees crawl all over me
tickling me tickling me everywhere and I like it this tickling
this sound of buzzing in my ears tickling on my eyelids in
my hair my shoulders the small of my back I can feel the
bees and I can hear them and I like it but I am scared too.
And in the distance I can hear the sound of a harmonica
the harmonica and the sound of trains and I say do
something but so softly   softly so the bees won't get angry
and there are more buzzing around me tickling me and I say
do something but I don't know who I am speaking to
anymore softly   so softly do   something something do
something softly   something softly   softly
do something.

□ □ □ □ ■

The train has a nickname Iron Horse that endears it
engenders it. These words recreate it make the train a living
thing whose eyes see only suggestions of images as they fly
past in focus out of focus. Train. That word so simple to say.
Who said a train is a train and not an Iron Horse anyway?

Isn't that always the way? One person says something and the next thing you know everybody is saying it.

■ ☐ ☐ ☐ ☐

Three times my father-in-law travelled to China to work. On his first trip he rode ten hours on a train from Beijing to Taiyuan. There were three classes of travellers   hard seat   soft seat   cabin. Not many outsiders journeyed to that area and it was thought he would not survive the trip if he travelled on the hard seats. So he was given a compartment and told to stay inside.

That first time he stayed three months and the people he worked with called him Old Horse.   Older experienced persons were called by this name and it was an honour. But it was also an honour to the sound of his name   Lo Mah   Lo Mah   Old Horse   Lo Mah.

Why are you working so hard Old Horse? they asked him. At your age you should be relaxing   gambling   taking it easy.

You must have a beautiful wife for you to come so far away from home and work so hard for her.

November 14, 1996 9:09 twelve cars   number 6441
travels slowly past us. We wait in our car in the cold and the
lights are red and hot and flashing in surprise to see
travellers on both sides of the red and white striped barriers.

Those staying and those moving on.

☐ ☐ ☐ ☐ ■

boxcars boxcars boxcars boxcars boxcars boxcars boxcars

☐ ☐ ☐ ☐ ■

Someone says a prayer for solitary souls travelling on a train.
Someone waits at the next stop   waits to hear the sound of
the train or

the sound of a solitary soul?

☐ ☐ ☐ ☐ ■

It was cold. It was cold in November in a small town on
the prairies cold. My grandmother had to leave town on the

train to have her fifth baby   her last baby. She waited in the hospital in Prince Albert for three weeks before she had a baby boy. She was kept in bed for ten days.

When she arrived back home she met my grandfather on the platform of the train station she handed him his son and fainted from weakness   from home sickness.

That line was closed years ago.

■ □ □ □ □

The train zips along the track. The train zips the track. The train is the pull that opens and closes the track opens and closes to infinity. There really is no end of the line. The line never ends. It goes on for someone else to places that may have already existed or have yet to become the line carries on to be discovered by chance   or opened deliberately by someone else some other time.

H after H after H after H the track breathes and sighs its own sound separate from the train after all.

■ □ □ □ □

Train tracks were built from one side of Canada to the other. Lines branched off so nothing would be left out.

But the lines were already there   were always there
tracks just made those lines visible   trying to claim space
trying to claim time.

□ □ □ □ ■

The train had a nickname and the ride did too. Riding the
rails. Stretches of track my grandfather travelled on. My
grandfather and thousands of others trying to find a place
that would offer them work. For all of them this place with
work was faceless and without a name. Work was what
would allow these men to stop moving along the tracks
trying to focus on narrow bands of light and dark   or closing
their eyes against them.

— We were going to get married anyway but   so now
we had a baby to feed and it was the beginning of the
depression just the beginning of it and there was no work.
So your grandfather rode the rails to look for work. He rode
from one side of the country to the other willing to do
anything. That's what you did   that's just what you did.
You tried to find work. As if it was a solid thing   something
real but it was just boxcars and the sound of those trains
running back and forth on the track.

■ ☐ ☐ ☐ ☐

A rigid grid   a rigid grid makes music   lines open to the sound of air. The lines guide the voice.

But there is a grid that breath and sound dissolve.

■ ☐ ☐ ☐ ☐

My mother and I took the train to Saskatoon. She was pregnant and thought it would be easier to make the trip before my sister was born. There was nothing to look at. Everything was moving too fast and I had to work too hard to focus on what was going past me outside the train. I crossed my eyes   slightly   so everything that passed me was blurred. There were only colours   light and dark bands lunging at me through the window of the train.

Blue   white   pink   green. I was starting to feel sick and when I closed my eyes   saw how my mother shook the green chenille bedspread over my bed at home   calming the swirls of pattern making the paisley tufts smooth. She folded the spread back over itself and lay my pillow just over the fold   just slightly   fluffed it and flipped the bedspread back. There was my pillow covered and tucked in perfectly and waiting there just for me.

I saw the cardboard Barbie my mother had cut from the back of a cereal box just that morning. I had asked her again which elf made which sound and she had told me again pointing to each word and sounding them out SNAP CRACKLE POP because I could never remember who made what sound. This cardboard Barbie wore a pink suit and a pink pillbox hat and pink high heels and pearls and I told my mother I would like a necklace just like that.

— When you're twenty-one you'll get my grandmother's engagement ring. It's still got the original pearl. It's a family heirloom a keepsake. Was that good? When my mother said *forpetesake* it never meant something good. I'd stick to wanting a pearl necklace like the one the doll wore.

I opened my eyes and asked my mother if I could sit on the inside and she said I could if I thought I wouldn't get sick. I just sat and looked down the aisle straight ahead so I wouldn't lose my balance. I thought I would lose my balance somehow and fall off the train and onto the tracks and no one would realize I was gone and I wouldn't be able to run fast enough to catch the train.

We were going to see my aunt in Saskatoon. She was a widow. She had *fits* and I asked how come and my mother told me when I was older she would tell me why just not now. She did tell me that just before my aunt had a fit she would smell oranges.

How the taste of the colour orange must have frightened her.

My aunt picked us up from the train station and it was the first and only time we visited her. She put us up for three days and the lamp beside my bed in her house had a shade the shape of a hoop skirt and I lay in bed thankful to be   still.

■ □ □ □ □

Stand under a train trestle.
The sound of a train sounds like birds frightened into flight.

■ □ □ □ □

Trains brought my ancestors to Saskatchewan. They had been factory workers in Germany and when they arrived in Canada an immigration official mistook an umlaut for two **i** s. It made no sense to him so he simply deleted what he thought was one half of the sound. An entire family instantly became different people in a different place   new eyes.

At that moment I became a different person too.

The lines of my ancestors   begin from many points. Denmark Germany Ireland Scotland and right here right here long before there were trains or tracks that claimed spaces that showed you the way.

Time was unmarked then but still it passed. Staying in one place or moving on   both became an attempt to claim it.

□ □ □ □ ■

When my great-grandparents found their homestead the section was all bush and no human sounds.

Were their words the first to be heard here between rocks and creek bed new leaves and fallen trees? Or were their words the first to be lost?

My great-grandparents had nothing to go back to anymore. Their home had disappeared lost and here they had found themselves   had reassembled and were trying to make spaces where none had existed.

They started to clear a space for their home to cut at the bush and pull stumps.

This place was to become their place a new home and they must make it respond to their words and their actions. This space was theirs. A piece of paper with their numbers marked it as theirs and they would become this place. The paper was proof.

■ □ □ □ □

The photographer told them, yes, there was a town in this direction and he pointed south before disappearing under his black hood. This photographer is the reason for the smile on my great-grandparents' faces for the smile on their four children's faces. His presence here meant the promise of other places and other people.

My grandmother cradles a bright orb in her four year-old hands.

— That was a yellow ball she would tell me years later. I had been allowed to bring one toy with me. I decided I would bring my yellow ball. So I held it up for the photographer because I was so proud I hadn't lost it on the boat or train.

— There is a town this way he told us.

So the path they created travelled in the direction of a photographer's gesture. They must create a straight line to a place where there would be other people a place to meet and talk and wonder at the stories of how they all came to be here.

My great-grandparents hacked and cut and believed they had made a claim believed they actually owned this land if for no other reason than to persuade themselves that what they had thought they were coming to was real. They wanted to buy flour and sugar and salt with the money they brought with them. Yes the money in their pocket was real. Even if their idea of claiming a space for their new home seemed only a strange dream.

□ □ □ □ ■

My great-grandfather looked at each tree as an affront to his choice to come here and he took his anger out on them. He had tried to steady a piece of wood as he brought down his axe so exhausted and sore and angry at his now irreversible choice and the place that was trying to overtake him blood poured from the ring finger on his left hand and he said nothing. My great-grandmother ran to help him offering up her skirt to wrap around his wound.

When she released him back to his work her skirt was soaked with his blood. She had had no blood for five months the folds of fabric now unable to hide her belly.

She shouted to my great-grandfather to stop just for a moment.

— I want my child to have a father with two hands she called out.

The poplars moved against her words and this infinite sky watched their dance.

Within four months she and the baby would be dead. Her own blood would have soaked through every white sheet and every white table cloth she had brought here. She would laugh at the absurdity as the midwife desperately tried to stop the flow of blood.

— This is not what I hoped to use these for she said to the woman.

The midwife shaking her head and feeling such pity for my great-grandmother and her dead baby. But also pity for the four small children she would be leaving behind in this strange place. They would have to make their own home now.

My mother worked in Banff for six weeks before she got married. She took the train to get there and said as soon as she got into the mountains she felt claustrophobic hemmed in   trapped. She worked as a waitress and stayed in a small apartment. There was one customer who fell in love with her and told her she shouldn't get married she should break her engagement and stay in Banff and marry him.

—He was just too nice always bringing me flowers telling me how beautiful I was. I couldn't wait to get out of there   I felt like I was going to suffocate.

After the six weeks I came back. I came back and   I felt ready to marry your father.

□ □ □ □ ■

Sitting upright on a train from Toronto to Edmonton my mother and brother rode across the Canadian shield. A country's impenetrable covering blasted and made flat for lines of track.

My family was travelling back home from Toronto skirting an airline strike. My father and I had managed to get seats on a plane   we beat the rest of us back.

I was seventeen years old and this was the last trip we would all make home together and it must have been a sign because we were already travelling a different route to a home we all believed to be a very different place.

My brother had an inner ear infection and for four days across four provinces he heard only the bass line of the train.

■ □ □ □ □

Music For Glass Harmonica. Music created for glasses filled with water. Music created from glasses filled with water.

Is it music for harmonica   at all? Or is it   armonica? This is not really music from a harmonica   it is music from glass it is music rising from water   rising H after H after H until the music itself changes state from glass   to water to vapour.

■ □ □ □ □

In Saskatchewan there was a town every ten miles. A new name a new place a new story. Sounds. Letters. Words. Stories moving so quickly through so much space we must strain to give them meaning.

When I was a kid my friend told me that if you put a
penny on the railroad track it would de-rail a train. We put
a penny on the tracks and ran.

I stayed awake a long time that night   after my mother
went to bed   after my father went to bed and the house was
dark. I lay there listening for the sound of the train
but all I heard was their muffled roaring.

Too much happiness cannot be trusted.

two

In this dim and wainscoted room is an old crock colour of sand polished and shining and ringed deep brown around its top. There is a small chip on its lip.

Dried eucalyptus is arranged just so and its scent is a sweet pungent green. The crock is marked Medalta Potteries.   My grandmother made sauerkraut in a crock like this.

Her crock had rested on a brown and orange vinyl covered chair in the corner of her dining room. Shards of cabbage cured in vinegar and salt and a bit of sugar were covered by a white china plate weighed down by a heavy grey stone.

— I had another one of these old crocks on the farm too she told me   I caught rainwater in it. The cows drank from it. One of the animals finally kicked it over and broke it. If I had known the thing was going to be worth something one day I would have brought it into the house.

When my grandmother was still a girl she moved with her father and her stepmother and her three new brothers and sisters to Medicine Hat. For more than a year she met her older brother under a trestle bridge halfway home to give him his lunch   mason jar of tea   brown sugar and lard sandwiches or sometimes a baked potato wrapped in a bleached flour bag.

Her brother was fourteen when he got work at Medalta. At the end of the day he was allowed to bring pieces home to paint.

My grandmother remembered sitting beside him at the kitchen table watching him paint a dog   dipping a small brush into brown pigment he mixed in a dented old muffin tin. The two of them said nothing   there could be no noise in the house while their father re-read the stories in old German newspapers his sister had sent him months ago. And so they sat silent   my grandmother imagining the taste of chocolate as the boy brought the clay dog to life by the yellow light of a kerosene lamp.

In the corner of this dim and wainscoted room is an old crock. Authentic medicine hat pottery the real thing my host tells me.

The walls are the colour of biscuits evenly golden and above the crock where walls and ceiling meet is a faint stain a spot where water is trying to find an entrance into this house. The stain is shaped like a bell hinting at the elements which could take over this house if they so choose. No. It is a calming thing this stain. It has a sound. Listen hard. There is a faint ringing a resonance soft and almost inaudible over the voices in this room.

These voices bump against each other and often laughter breaks away from the random movement of these human sounds and fading adopts the bell's tone but only for an instant. I am silent and this union of sound goes unnoticed by the others in the room it is played just for me. This is the taste of purple the taste of an instant when voice and hum meet a memory of when clay water and air mix a silk silt brushing skin a deep wine an earthy taste on the tongue just before swallowing taking warmth into my body.

Once I thought this pink house belonged to me   but we were just renting. Uneven sidewalk out to the back fence where asparagus grew precious and tall but my mother didn't know what asparagus was back then. She had never seen it before.

The asparagus transformed into green froth growing well past the top of the white picket fence so clean and fresh and perfect. Running beside the fence was a bed of flowers my mother had planted daisies bachelor buttons marigolds. One day

one summer she filled a rubber blow-up pool and my sister and I waited until the sun warmed the water. We stuck our feet in and out quickly my sister copying my movements her short legs barely able to reach over the three red coils that were the pool's walls.

When the water was warm we pretended we could swim raising our arms over our heads and kicking our feet. My mother sat constantly beside the pool.

— You can drown in a cup of water.
We squirted the pool water out of our mouths like we had seen cartoon characters do.

— Don't do that the water's dirty my mother said.
But we had scooped the bugs out and now the water just tasted warm and smelled like a brand new doll.

There is a picture of me in the backyard of the pink house.
I can feel the wind on the surface of the photograph.

Me. Knee-length houndstooth coat and white gloves. It
was windy and April. It was my birthday and there was no
flash on the camera so the picture had to be taken outside
where there was light enough to create an image. But I
couldn't smile for a picture. I was looking for the noise of big
semis speeding north down 66th street past the Santa Rosa
Grocery with its black shingled roof its grey shingled walls
and I was trying to keep separate the sounds of the other
children and the sound of my mother telling me

— Look this way. Look over here.

and the sound of her snapping her fingers above her head
and the sound of my friends calling my name and the sound
of the cocker spaniel next door barking through the pickets
and the sound of my sister's patent leather shoes on the
cement sidewalk and the sound of the radio left on the
kitchen counter.

It was impossible. The noise of those trucks was all
I could hear.

Police are seeking the whereabouts of:

Pick anywhere you like. Pick anyone you like.

Last seen:

Pick any place you like. Go ahead pick a place and I will long for it to be home.

■ □ □ □ □

— Lie down and go to sleep my mother tells me.

This room seems big and the floor is smooth with shiny green tiles that we now all cover   ourselves covered in blankets sheets and pillows. I would think back to this room years later and I would feel happy. My grandmother tucked a sheet over the curtain rod on the window that was big and high above my head. I would think back to this room years later and I would feel happy even though my father described us then as a bunch of DPs.

What would anyone have seen if they had bothered to look in the window? Rows of bodies covered with sheets heads all pointing in the direction from which they had come like the aftermath of some natural disaster you could see on TV any night of the week.

□   □   □   □   ■

My mother and father had moved twice by the time I turned two. The third time we moved out of Saskatchewan to Edmonton so my father could find work.

— When we have $5000 we'll move back he told me. And of course we had made that and more but by that time we had stopped talking about it.

My mother knew what she longed for had vanished. What she hoped for would never happen.

You can convince yourself of anything.

Concrete poured from the mouth of the cement truck. My father spread it with a blunt square shovel quickly in-between the basement forms. Putting in basements waiting for cement trucks hoping it wouldn't rain before the cement had time to dry my father set the foundations of other people's homes. If the basement cracked it would let in water. A leaky basement a leaky foundation the elements waiting to come in. This had to be done right the first time.

His back ached. He had fallen from the second floor of an apartment his crew had been framing right onto a pile of hard snow. In bed for two days. Two days' lost wages in the dead of winter.

Every so often he would be reminded. Every so often his back would ache and he would be reminded of working in the cold 30 below. He would be reminded of the fall. Hard snow. His boots lined with newspaper. The cigarette he had only just lit. Trying to regain his balance. Wondering if the bruise had ever really healed. He hoped he would never fall like that again. One fall like that was enough. If he fell like that again well he just might not get back up.

Things changed after that fall. Nothing anyone else would notice like the shift in the magnetic poles when north becomes south and south becomes north. Things lined up differently on the inside pointed in a different direction. It was nothing anyone else would notice. When my father was at home with us he had a different face he never laughed he rarely even spoke.

— What are you doing Dad? Him at the kitchen table smoking and looking out the window at the sky.

— Thinking.

        □ □ □ □ ■

The Fear of Power Tools:

The scree of metal cutting through wood the skeleton of a house the bones of a family's life being built or dismantled or destroyed.

This is truly a phobia: sanders nail guns jig saws drills skill saws. It could be just simple *fear*: of blood severed bone a stub of finger growing a tiny nail its root searching for the missing digit. A severed finger moving with a life of its own. Afraid of that tiny nail growing out the top and forgetting the root of nail trying to remember where the finger began when it was just a small nub growing underwater in the womb.

■ ☐ ☐ ☐ ☐

A smooth blue sky can seem to trap you sometimes
weigh down on you like deep water. You are below the
surface. You are drowning. This is a recurring dream a
fiction that finds you returning to a place that stops your
breath. Stops feeling.

■ ☐ ☐ ☐ ☐

It was not the sun my grandmother sought refuge from
going inside after working out in the garden. It was the sky
itself too big too heavy even the clouds could not cut the
incessant blue.

■ ☐ ☐ ☐ ☐

On the cement patio in the backyard his daughter bent
over a nail jutting out from a small scrap of 2 x 4 frantically
she tried to pound the nail into the wood with a heavy
round rock trying to mimic the image she had of her father
at work. She could summon the picture of him pounding in
nail after nail pinning down boards or sheets of wood
creating floors or roofs bringing a house to life. He made

home building look so easy she believed it to be magic   and

she would recreate his spell   break it down into its parts

hammer   wood   the quick movement of her father's arm as

he brought the hammer to the nail pounding it into the

wood in only two hits. He always found his mark. The quick

staccato of the steel head of the hammer hitting the head of

the nail quickly followed by the thud of the hammer hitting

wood. A perfect hit.

— What are you doing to that nail?

— Hitting it with a wock.

— With a what?

— A wock.

— A what?

— A wock.

— What?

— I'm hitting it with a stone.

— Say rock again.

— No.

The girl's father laughed touched the top of her head as

he walked toward the pile of 2 x 4s on the grass just beyond

the patio. She stopped pounding momentarily and looked

up as he passed balancing several long pieces of lumber on

his shoulder. Letting the back door slam. His work boots on the back steps. She went back to pounding. The roundness of the rock made it difficult for her to hit the nail on the head. But she would do it. She was after that sound of a perfect hit. A popping sound   not the scrape of stone metal that meant she had missed   again.

■ ☐ ☐ ☐ ☐

In the spring when the snow began to melt we would collect the tiniest rocks as if they were exquisite small jewels. We were going to set up a stand and sell them   lemonade too.

— Who would buy the rocks anyway?
— *Passerbys.* The gold rush started by luck didn't it?

Picking the prettiest little pebbles   offering them up. We would start a gold rush right on our street.

Steele Heights Edmonton. We thought it was steel   hard steel. Hard and strong and high. Hit the heights. We didn't know until we went to school that it was the name of some soldier. I found out later he had fought against Louis Riel.

When our parents bought the lot in Steele Heights it was not called that at all. It was called Honeymoon Village. We didn't know at the time what a honeymoon was. We thought it must be something happy.

☐ ☐ ☐ ☐ ■

What was left were broken clumps of bare earth. At this time of year the rock garden had a wide open scared look. Braced to scream   funny   she got as much satisfaction from removing the flowers as she did planting them watching them spread colour in between the rocks   trying to overtake the hard stone   change it in some way. But that was silly. Whoever looked at the garden changed it   not the flowers. The perception of the flowers made that garden what it was.

She had broken each rock herself   had collected them since they first began building the house seven years earlier. Rows of sharp teeth   two-tiered and bordered by the front cement step. You had to pass by these rocks if you followed the sidewalk to the back door.

Even if their idea of claiming space for their new home seemed only a strange dream.

Sometimes she found dead birds in the dirt on the top row of the rock garden   fooled by the large picture window directly above   thinking it was a passageway through a quick fly-by. She had heard somewhere that glass actually moved   the molecules never stopped. Maybe the birds were tricked by the window's false stillness   the house's false calm.

If one of her children found a dead bird first she would hold a mock funeral. Empty a Q-tip box   line it with tissue place the bird tenderly inside   then with the children crying the bird would be buried in the backyard. A hymn *all things bright and beautiful*   yes, there is a heaven for birds.

If her children hadn't seen it first   she would quickly scoop the hard thing up with a shovel and throw it in the garbage.

■ ☐ ☐ ☐ ☐

She straightened slowly. Her back hurt   she could swear that at times the vertebrae scraped against each other separate little pebbles stacked one on top the other. She arched her back shaping those pebbles into a **C**.

No wonder birds hit the window   that glass was spotless. No little fingerprints   certainly no streaks. She could see right through to the inside of her house   the pumpkin-coloured chair the interior decorator had said would tie in the brown sofa   beige drapes   gold swivel chair the kids used to play merry-go-round.

The wall dividing the living room and dining room doubled as a planter   halfway down ivy began its helical ascent up narrow slats and was pinned to the wall with Scotch Tape as it grew beyond its confines.

□   □   □   □   ■

We scoured the ditch for rocks   on the incline we arranged them in our initials   and circled the letters in stone then we ran down the hill through the ditch and across the road   trying to gain footing on the shifting gravel. We stood on the opposite edge of the road   looked at the letters a smiling mouth we had made from stones.

This was a vow by my parents   they had named themselves under the sky beside the road   leading to and from both their houses. They had thought they would stay there forever. They had named themselves. This act made them

a part of their journey   the beginning of their own story and
anyone else driving along this road would see those letters
and unless they chose to stop in the same place   stop in the
same place and rearrange the stones   the letters signifying
my parents would always be there   settled right into the
scruffy ditch.

We put our arms around each other and walked back to
the car.

— Let's always be like this I said.

Laughing as we peeled down the road   gravel battering
the metal bowels of the car and shooting out behind us
along with big clouds of dust.

■   ☐   ☐   ☐   ☐

My grandmother opened the lid of her jewellery box. It
was meant to look like a treasure chest but it was only cheap
tin. When she got it for Christmas a long time before it had
been full of chocolates. Now it held two necklaces   one of
plastic beads a strand of black and white and some fake
pearls intermittent on a gold chain and three earrings

lacking mates. She also kept a lipstick in that box the only one she owned. It was a bloodbright red the kind that had been in fashion a long time ago the kind of red you cannot bear to give up to whims or airs. When she painted with it the colour itself became her lips and gave her face a quality that made it seem capable of things altogether beyond the possibilities of her everyday.

There was a dance at the legion hall and she was going with my grandfather and my parents and I was excited as I watched all of them walking out the back door. It was still hot from the day and they all passed under the empty sagging clothesline in the dressiest clothes they owned. My mother and my grandmother were walking on the balls of their feet trying to keep their high heels from sinking into the silty sand. It seemed as if they were trying to walk quietly straining to keep from waking anyone trying not to make a sound.

□ □ □ □ ■

The house in Steele Heights had hardwood floors and after my mother had waxed them she had us sit on a blanket pulling us around the room to bring a shine to the floors.

And the sun shone on us as she pulled us back and forth trying to hold on to the sides of the yellow blanket laughing and falling off and chasing my mother to grab hold of the blanket pretending we were late for the train and getting on just in time.

■ ☐ ☐ ☐ ☐

My grandmother rode the Greyhound from Saskatchewan once to stay with us for awhile   she told us she was on a little holiday. She told my mother she was leaving and not going back because nobody appreciated her anyway.

— I'm thinking I'll go up north   cook in a camp I heard her say while she and my mother sat at the kitchen table smoking.

I wonder if she knew she was dying that this might be her last chance to get away her last chance at   something.

But she went back home in the end.

— You grow fond of someone after all those years she said.

There were some girls from the neighbourhood inside watching TV. It was summer and that time just after supper and before bed. It was summer and any kind of school day routine was knocked on the head. We could have gone outside and played kick the can or hide and seek but everyone it seemed had decided to go to Jill's and watch TV. I had never been asked inside but when I rang the bell and asked if Jill could come out to play Jill asked her mother if I could come in this once.

— She can come in if she behaves herself Mrs. Jenkins said. I didn't know what I had done or what she thought I might do.

I found a spot on the rug which Mrs. Jenkins called *carpet* suddenly conscious of just how dirty my feet were and I could see Mrs. Jenkins looking at them. I tried to tuck them under me but she had already seen them and I realized my clothes were dirty too from a day playing outside my hair had come away from the braid my mother wove down my back. I wished I had never gone to that door in the first place. But I was frozen in that spot conspicuous as a statue with no voice and no way out.

The living room of the house in Steele Heights had a brown couch and matching chair.

— It's been peed on puked on and jumped on and it still looks good my mother said.

There was a raised pattern in the couch like pineapples. I would come to love this pattern   paisley   after overhearing my mother talk to the interior decorator she looked up in the yellow pages.

What the decorator had to start with was the brown couch and a matching chair.   Over the couch was a velvet painting of mountains and pine trees with a river in the foreground. I had touched this picture many times. The paint was hard and the velvet yielded when I poked it. There was also a gold swivel chair we played merry-go-round on and a planter between the living room and dining room. Ivy climbed the wooden spindles.

The interior decorator did not stay long. She recommended a pumpkin colour occasional chair which my mother found and bought and placed against a living room

wall. Nothing much changed really.

— It was a total waste of money I heard my mother tell

a friend.

I stuck the tines of a fork through the loops of the couch's

synthetic fabric and pulled hard. The material refused to

break.

□ □ □ □ ■

Ian and Sylvia sang a song about going out to Alberta to

find work and the first time I heard it I thought it was just

like what my family did   only my mother hadn't stayed

behind and we came too.

When my oldest son was little I sang that song for him

while he was drifting into sleep.

— Why is it songs about people loving each other are

always sad? he asked.

I didn't have the heart at that moment to tell him that Ian had actually come out to Alberta. I still don't know if he ever offered to send Sylvia the fare.

■ □ □ □ □

You try to remember when or where it all might have begun and you really can't figure it out. Was it a moment a certain day of the week? A month before you noticed   or a whole year that you just put up with something. You make up excuses to forget you reconcile with someone else with yourself and you carry on. Because nothing ever really begins nothing ever really ends. You might only be able to pinpoint one moment of recognition and after awhile even that jagged fragment becomes smoother and easier to close inside your hand.

■ □ □ □ □

We chose our son's name travelling through Ireland in a little red Fiat with no radio.   I had written a list of girls' names and a list of boys' names. There our choices seemed to have a meaning rooted in that country. How would these names fit when we came back to Canada   that cold new and endless country?

In the moment our son is born we recognize him and so too his name. Time instantly rearranges itself. What came before seems to have also included him. His name   his presence asserts itself in every place I have ever been.

□ □ □ □ ■

Recurring dream:

there is a house. Its front is made entirely of glass and the lights shine out as stars illuminating staircases which criss-cross the infinite levels of the house. I ring the front bell and a man I know from somewhere answers. He says nothing but lets me in. I stare at his dark hair his sad mouth and blue eyes and close the door behind me.

□ □ □ □ ■

Underneath the steps leading to the suite above my grandparents' was a crawlspace. It was locked from the outside with a metal clip that looked like a rusty butterfly and inside the space smelled like damp concrete and wet earth and in it were wooden frames and bicycle wheels shovels a hoe and a rake.

In this space was the past life of every person whose face came towards me when we were driving in the car   fading as we passed. I believed that here were the souls of everyone I would never call by name.

■ □ □ □ □

What is left to mark what my father built? Basements he poured and wooden frames he constructed are all hidden and forgotten   pieces of him that will never be found. There are no monuments but   somewhere blueprints must exist for what he built in the 60s and 70s when entire communities sprang up from holes in the ground. When houses and sidewalks began creeping into farmers' fields and from our backyard we could still see cows eating grass.

Home is a myth.

We are seeking the whereabouts of:

The family set out for:

Last seen:

A basement suite in Prince Albert Saskatchewan a main floor rented in Saskatoon a basement suite in Edmonton. Go ahead pick a place and I will long for it to be home.

Home is a myth.

three

The abbreviated version
would be to describe the moment not days not years that
occurred to get to this place and others like it. With my
fingers on black and white keys wanting to put them to
good use   wanting my fingers to make sense of the sound
hanging in the air   a baby's soul waiting to be born.

— Do you remember how to play it? my father asks.

He is out of character dressed in a cardigan clean
pressed dress shirt and *slacks*. We have been invited to a
party for subcontractors and their families given by the
president of the company my father sometimes works for
pouring basements   framing houses.

The president's house has two tall white columns in front and brick around the heavy paneled wood door. His daughter's room has been *decorated* in pink and there are white fluffy slippers at the foot of her bed. The president and his family have their piano in the *rec room.*

I can't remember how to play it. I can't remember how to read the music. I don't know where the notes are anymore.

My father was calm and quiet as he stood over me with a drink in his hand. He wanted so badly for me to remember how to play.

— I can't.
— If you remember call me   he said and patted my head stepping softly up the stairs in brand new black nylon socks.

I sat at the piano wanting remembrance   but not understanding why.

■ ☐ ☐ ☐ ☐

— We're getting rid of the piano. You don't practise   my mother said.

Our piano was an upright. A converted *player piano* an instrument that had once created music from the open spaces on a roll of paper.

It was a huge presence in the room up against the wall where the brown couch used to be. When the sun shone through the picture window the sunlight made a picture shiny bare hardwood floors framed in the thick black shadows of the piano legs.

My mother had crocheted a white doily in a pineapple pattern for the top and its lace pattern hung down pointing accusingly at my open music book.

The piano was so heavy it was making the floor underneath it buckle. It was taking up too much space so my parents bought a stereo that was only ever tuned to one radio station and played the six records we owned in rotation.

When the piano first came my mother said she wanted us to have the chances she never had my father said nothing.

□ □ □ □ ■

Frost collected on one corner of my bedroom window and in the winter silence before my father got up for work I was happy. The furnace exhaled its comforting breath and I got out of bed to plug in the green plastic radio on the floor beside my bed then scrambled back under the blankets. The music was beautifully distant and tinny   *winchester cathedral you could have done something.*

■ ☐ ☐ ☐ ☐

My sister and I put macaroni and water in a tupperware tumbler and tried to cook it over the heat register under our brother's crib. We stirred the alternately hard and slimy mess and were going to eat it just to see...

— Get out from under there you two don't wake up your brother. You can't eat raw macaroni it'll swell up in your stomach like a balloon and make   you sick.

■ ☐ ☐ ☐ ☐

In winter the grey felt insoles of our boots seemed always to rest on heat registers   looking like remnants of spontaneous human combustion and yet on their own they resembled nothing human at all.

My mother darned my father's wool work socks using a rubber ball to help recreate the worn-out heels. She knit special mitts for him   shaping a thumb and index finger so

he could hold a nail even in snow even in the wind. These
strange creations looked to be for something other than my
father   an amphibious creature straddling land and sea
craving both water and sky.

□   □   □   □   ■

Winter. It seemed like my father hadn't worked for a
long time.

— It costs more money for a bulldozer to rip frozen
ground up   he said. No one wants to build when it's this
goddamn cold.

Flat carpenter's pencils sharpened with the butcher knife
sat on the counter by the phone   waiting for someone to call
with work.

For breakfast we ate puffed wheat or bread with milk and
sugar. Why was it okay to eat something that was puffed up
outside your stomach and not okay to eat something that
puffed up *inside* your stomach?

My grandfather believed that UFOs existed and bought magazines to prove it. I kept my bedroom curtains closed at night so aliens would not be able to peer in and kidnap me if they ever landed on our front lawn. I stopped closing my curtains when we moved away from the city.

Aliens would never be able to find me in the darkness of the country now I would be invisible from outer space.

We parted grass where the dog had been jumping and
found a mouse nest   squirming pink with small hairless
creatures. We could feel the warmth coming from them.
The mother was nowhere to be found she must have run off
when she heard us. We couldn't stop the dog from eating
the poor things.

□ □ □ □ ■

— Now tell me about when you were little.

My sister grasps for a story to tell her children
something happy   something she is happy to give them like
an heirloom passed from generation to generation.

— There was this time I must have been about three. I sat
on the back cement step with our dog at my feet and I was
eating peanut butter on toast it was warm and melting. The
sun shone on my legs and I remember feeling a quiet
happiness.

— It must have been only a few minutes she tells me.

This is what she remembers and I believe her.

four

There was a train in my great-grandfather's living room.

It travelled inside a lamp cylindrical and blanket stitched top and bottom with a narrow brown plastic lace. On the shade there was a train billowing smoke. It was an old-fashioned train the kind you see on old westerns or in thick books of bedtime stories.

When the lamp was turned on the train moved. My great-grandfather laughed at my fascination.

— It's the bulb inside child. See? It's turning around and around.

I didn't care about his explanation. I saw the train moving moving silently around the shade moving endlessly around that room while my great-grandmother sat perpetually in her chair.

Her hands her legs her mouth trembled uncontrollably and the clear plastic buttons that travelled from the neck of her black and white polka-dot dress moved along the contours of her body taken along with the rhythm of her breathing.

My great-grandfather always treated me to white marshmallows when I visited and even though I never ate them at home   I never really liked the taste of them   there somehow in that place they were transformed and became something different once inside my mouth. I stood in front of the small square table where the train travelled past a china bird perched on a branch and the small porcelain figure of a girl Made In Occupied Japan and I ate that white marshmallow believing that it tasted of the train's soft sweet smoke   obscure and faraway as growing old.

five

My grandmother must believe in an afterlife. She must also believe in reincarnation life after death and life after life. She lay in her bed propped on pillows with mismatched pillowcases melting into the patterns of the fabric itself the methodically rigid angles of the plaid surreal orange and brown petals.

Here the bedclothes are dusted with the silt of sleep and sickness lack of dreams   of desire. Here there is no virtue to be found in the past. Memory's infidelity is the ultimate betrayal.

My grandmother is dying her breath stolen by the air around her and she can no longer fight to keep it. It takes a monumental effort simply to speak.

Fri Mar 20

I was trying to watch TV & just couldn't get into it. So as I owe you a letter here goes. It's snowing & cold here we've been spoiled after all the nice weather we've had. I keep on the go. Grampa was wanting to go to town the other day & I didn't want to go. So I said to him (go find something to do). So he went out & started burning grass. I decided to go lay down. He came in & sat down. All at once I heard him say (For Christ's sake) & run outside. I jumped up & run out thru the mud & he'd burnt up the Bunk House & there was a granary of Rape beside it. I shovelled snow & threw water till I was tired. I had a laugh when we got it in control. I told him I didn't expect to get so damn busy all of a sudden.

Water in a chipped white china bowl. The bowl rests on the yellow and silver star-specked arborite kitchen counter and she dips her fingers into stillness turned warm from the heat and sprinkles it over the sleeve of his white shirt. The cloth makes a soft sizzling sound as the iron passes over its stark white.

Steam rises listlessly when she sets the iron upright on the board covered with small pink flowers. The iron releases the scent of soap and reminds her of what he smelled like when he had asked her to dance and she had put her face as close to him as she dared in public and breathed quiet and deep to remember the scent of him.

A wasp butts angrily against the window he can find no way inside. She turns to the sound and wonders where the nest might be. A nest of white paper with only a small opening to go in and out. Sprinkling the cuff of the shirt with water and slowly drawing the tip of the iron in and out of the sleeve itself she smiles at the wasp's frustration.

□ □ □ □ ■

She rode her horse bareback to school every morning. Every morning she was late getting to that small yet monumental building: white with a bright red shingled roof and three steps up to the front door. The two windows on either side of the front steps looked like checkerboards and the shadowed faces of the children seen from a distance were like pieces in the game.

She took off her horse's bridle rubbed the length of its black nose then patted his neck and shouted: HOME DOLLIE. She watched her horse until it disappeared over the hill and turned to face the door.

— Agatha Somerville what is your excuse today?

— I noticed the roses Mr. Poole.

— The roses? You mean those sparse and sorry *excuses* for roses don't you Agatha?

— No I mean the pink roses the wild ones.

— I'm telling you now you do not know what a real rose looks like Agatha.

— I believe I do Mr. Poole. I see them everywhere.

— They are more akin to weeds than roses I'm afraid.

— Pardon me Mr. Poole but they aren't weeds. They're flowers.

— Well Agatha, you are now free at my behest to notice what passes for roses here for the remainder of the day if you so wish. You are dismissed.

— But Mr. Poole, I've already sent my horse...

— Then it will be waiting for you when you arrive home.

She stared at the red knot that held together the teacher's stiff white collar. Imagining she was still holding onto the bridle holding onto the image of that red knot she started to hum softly and turned her eyes up to the flag. A red cross and more red criss-crossing and still more red and now she was singing at the top of her voice in the dead silence of the twenty other students who were staring straight ahead what the hell were they looking at?

— God save our gracious King long live our gracious King God save our King

The teacher did nothing to stop her singing. She knew he would do nothing to stop her. He was fixed to his spot by that same duty and allegiance he drummed into his students every day. She continued to stare at the red knot of his tie after she had finished singing. How the stripes on his tie imitated the lines on the flag.

A grid that breath and sound dissolve.

She lit a white candle and dripped wax onto a chipped china saucer. The wax pooled in the shadowed place meant for the matching cup but the matching cup had been broken. She couldn't remember when. Matching china and polished silver stopped being so important after her mother died but she did remember this particular cup. It had been her mother's favourite. The inside of the cup was hand painted with ochre flowers and a narrow black filigree on a pale yellow band. There had been a narrow gold stripe around the lip. The saucer had those same ochre flowers and filigree but the narrow gold stripe was fading away.

— This is fine bone china. I prefer to drink my tea from bone china. See? When I hold it up to the lamp I can see my hand through it.

She remembered a time before her mother had been sick the silhouette of her mother's fingers a shade's shadow. She pressed the bottom of the candle into the white wax and held it there until the candle could stand on its own.

My grandmother took an egg from the basket on the table and raised it up to the yellow of the flame. A tiny crack became so obvious in front of the fire but away it seemed a perfect egg. She held it between her thumb and middle finger like a precious icon and gently set it in a large brown crockery bowl lined with a white tea towel.

She took another egg from the basket and raised it to the candle. A spot. She gagged and when she covered her mouth with her hand dropped the egg to the floor.

— It has to be true then she thought trying to fight her own churning stomach. What will I tell Father?

She blew out the candle.

□ □ □ □ ■

These are not church walls but the walls of a small house built on a hill and facing east. These are the walls of a house made real by the movement of a soapy rag held in a fist. This movement across and down the pale yellow walls is the will to believe that anything is still possible that here still something could begin and something could end.

These walls have a plaster skin made of horse hair and sand. In these walls animals run. In these walls are endless grains of sand and as this girl wipes these walls she wants to believe that to make them come clean will in some way restore her and this house to the way it was before everything.

These are the walls she now dreams about every night. They speak to her with her mother's voice but it is a language she cannot understand. She wants so desperately to find the meaning of the words and goes to bed earlier each night waiting for sleep to come. Waiting for the words that she might finally understand the words that would tell her what she must do.

— What's wrong with you Aggie? Her father asks. His fear of an answer he already knows.

He feels no anger towards his daughter his only child and anyone who could feel ashamed of her now is an ocean away or dead. Weeks to receive his letter weeks to receive a reply. He could send word to his sister that Aggie had been married and after the baby has been born lie about the birth date. Nobody need ever know.

She would be saved. There was still time for him to save her.

Her father saves silver in a tobacco tin under his bed. She could easily empty it and maybe ask the hired man to hitch the horses and take her to town. He would do it for her she is certain without asking why. She could wait for the train it came through town at eight o'clock every night. Like clockwork. In the winter she heard the whistle when she was reading in her room. The sound carried all the way from town.

    Over wood

               and wire fences

                      over taut clotheslines

over gravel roads   sloughs

        farms   bush

                and drifted fields

right to her room. The train could carry her even farther. And nobody would ever know.

six

My grandparents' basement suite was near a train yard. Empty cars were stacked green and orange and silver and marked with letters I knew by now but just couldn't put together names symbols. These marks said all that need be said. These marks could tell me all I would ever need to know. The train yard was the story of where my grandparents had come from and where they were now. It was also the story of where I came from and might one day be going.

Their yard was separated from the north-end neighbourhood by a chain link barbed wire topped fence. The neighbourhood was a neatly laid-out collection of duplexes and houses that had suites top and bottom with wrought iron railings linking the top suites to the ground. Leading to the basement suites were concrete steps that disappeared into shadows.

Inside the train yard the tracks ran straight and curved into each other making the same kind of marks my skate blades made on ice in winter. Tracks made it look so easy to leave an impression on the earth.

— Let's make tracks out of here.

I always looked for the red and white striped windsock. Why did trains need to know which way the wind was blowing?

■　□　□　□　□

Cut marks into trees on your way. We create our own pattern our own   marks. Cut marks so that I can find the way.

■　□　□　□　□

My father comes from a place where winter moves into people's consciousness a solid block of grey   big   against the sky.

He comes from a time when water was something you caught or saved in crocks or barrels or bare hands. He comes from a place where fire was needed as much as feared.

Last seen:

The walls of the apartment building were like three-dimensional Mondrian paintings. Their asymmetry was constructed on the apartment's plywood floor and raised to create the illusion of a place where people would soon live. Through the open spaces of the walls were framed portions of sky. I so wanted to look out those spaces before they turned into glass windows. I wanted to look out those spaces across to the train cars stacked in the trainyard.

I was not to go near construction sites they were fraught with nails and glass and things that could fall on my head. I had been warned. But it was Sunday and I wasn't really far from our house and the morning had been so quiet.

A 2 x 12 stretched across the basement's open trench. I could smell the scent of new wood and wanted to discover it wanted to look out the spaces the pieces of wood made and imagine my life in them.

All I had to do was walk across the narrow board the trench wasn't really that wide. I could just walk across this board and I could look across the street and see straight to the train yard. I would be as high as the cars. It was so quiet. I could hear only a soft humming and the board was stretching over the trench steel rebar jutting out from the basement still not back filled.

I couldn't make myself walk along the narrow plank. I straddled the board and slid slowly over the trench slid slowly and tried to focus on the place where the door would be the openings where the windows would be. These spaces were nothing but inevitability of doors of windows indicators of where things would end up.

I inched across the 2 x 12 and reached the floor of the apartment spreading my fingers wide on the wood and kneeling on the very scent of a new building. The windows were almost too high for me to see out but when I stood on my toes and stretched I could see through the open spaces through the possibility of glass to the houses where other families lived and I could look directly across to them. They seemed only empty and quiet.

I thought I must be the last person on earth and if I was I could live in any house I wanted to. I could even make my home in one of those train cars and I sure wouldn't care which way the wind was blowing.

— Why are there always walls in houses? my four-year-
old son asks   one of those questions whose answer you have
long ago accepted and now cannot remember a time when
you even wondered about such things.

— They keep things separate   tell you what to do in
what space.

— You can lean against them too   or draw on them
he says.

■ ☐ ☐ ☐ ☐

What is it that brings us to someplace   some place? A place to begin   a place to end up. Some place is where my grandmother's mother ended up. From Ireland crossing an ocean. From Halifax crossing a country to someplace that made her captive. Oh yes there was a house   in it folded in the drawer of a stately dark wood hutch were her linens precious   starched   white.

This is a house   her house with a narrow set of stairs that lead to the room where she will die. A house in the middle of things   in the middle of a field at the end of the road at the top of a hill. A room in the middle of nowhere.

In this house a woman dies slowly the small lump she discovered under her left arm growing to take over her body and leaving only pain in its place. There was nothing anyone could do.

There was nowhere anyone could go. There was only waiting.

■ ☐ ☐ ☐ ☐

My grandmother was forced to look at her mother's body after she died. After months of being told to stay away

because she was very sick and in terrible pain and needed to
just rest she was finally allowed to remain beside her own
mother as long as she wanted.

— Kiss her goodbye now child. You'll never get another
chance the aunt said.

She couldn't bring herself to touch her. Her own mother
and she couldn't bring herself to touch her skin. She had
nothing to say to her no thoughts about this woman or
herself at all.

— Say your piece to her. But my grandmother thought
her aunt meant *peace* and so that is the only word she
whispered. It was too late now to say goodbye anyway. She
wished she had been allowed to say that when her mother
could have heard her.

— Better to remember her the way she was before than to
remember her as she is her aunt said.

There was no remembrance of what her mother had been
before this point. What had her voice sounded like? What
was the colour of her eyes? She tried to remember the smell
of her mother's hands as she fastened the top button of the
sailor coat she had made for her. The only thing she could
remember was the shadow of her mother's fingers moving

behind a china plate. Her mother's fingers moving with the blurred opacity of something not quite real.

So now she sat underneath the open window of her mother's room. The curtains were still in the dry hot air. Her aunt's soft crying.

— She was so young too young.

All along this side of the house her mother had planted baby's breath. Small black insects darted from white flower to white flower. These flowers grew in sickeningly sweet wisps that were thick and tangled and diaphanous at the same time. My grandmother pulled every one out by the root.

■ □ □ □ □

Every place exacts a price so why stay? An undetermined length of time a minute a while   several years a lifetime a life sentence.

Police are seeking the whereabouts of:

Pick a person a set of features a sound you remember a scent sensation of skin.

They were going home. They were on their way home. They were making their way back home.

Home keeps coming back to me again and again a recurring dream a recurring theme a recurring fiction.

Home does not exist. Home is a myth.

□ □ □ □ ■

The official cause of my grandmother's death was a blood clot in the lung. But it was her heart that finally gave out. It had simply been forced to work too hard.

seven

Illuminations:

Pas de deux. Dancers' movements outlined in light.
Their images follow each other in an infinite flow of
muscles and bones a gesture drawing come to life on the
television screen.

Try to follow the dance dancer dancers.

— How do they do that, mom?

— It's just a camera trick.

But how can camera tricks account for the things that
end up inside the screen? How many tricks occur outside
the screen?

Try to follow the dance dancer dancers.

The image on the screen projects onto the image of yourself in front of the screen. You have become that blue glow. You are the screen. You become the image inside the screen the image on the margin of a sheet of paper. This is just a crude version of yourself stiff and smiling or loose and smiling. Here you are part of the story after all.

■ ☐ ☐ ☐ ☐

Illuminations:

The image of your first son's face opening on the world. The sound of your second son's cry opening into silence. The first time your child says your name. The first time you realize you will one day lose them.

You are allowed to watch your own life. A sudden and unexpected opening occurs that makes something one small thing make sense. But just as quickly the opening closes around you. The darkness is so dense there remains only a fading outline of light the fast fading outline of knowlege.

A camera trick.

Wedding Photograph: My grandmother and grandfather were beautiful on their wedding day. There wasn't a trace of the future on their faces.

My grandfather was wearing a black suit and a serious look on his face. My grandmother was wearing a satin dress she had made herself cut on the bias the kind a 30s movie star would wear and a white veil that was attached to a chain of yellow daisies that circled her head. She carried a bouquet of wildflowers she had picked herself before the ceremony beyond the small patch of mowed grass behind her house. Her shoes white satin slippers with tiny flowers embroidered across the toe were entirely ill-suited to her but her aunt had insisted.

— What are you going to do? Get married in bare feet?

— Why not? My grandmother said and she had laughed.

☐ ☐ ☐ ☐ ■

— Get back in here Aggie, you don't want him to see you it's bad luck her aunt shouted at her. What do you want with a bunch of weeds anyway?

— I want to hold something. Look at the colours

and she held up the bunch of flowers for her aunt to see and

it was at this moment that her future husband my grandfather

came over the crest of the rutted road that led to her house.

Dust puffed up from the hooves of the horse that drew his

buggy. He was wearing the only suit he would ever own it

was black and his two brothers were wearing mismatched

jackets and trousers.

My grandmother looked straight at him and her first

thought was that she would take a flower from those she

picked and pin it to his lapel.

The people who were gathered in the yard the women

anyway started to shout that my grandmother should run

inside quickly get inside but instead of running she just

stood there. It was too late. She had seen him. He had seen

her. Shading her eyes with her free hand she waved at my

grandfather with her bouquet. An act so unashamed so

unflinching that the crowd laughed softly at the sheer

spontaneity of the gesture.

Oh perhaps she was waving to warn him.

Snow still on the ground but the scent of thawing earth seeps from under the cold. Winter is dying.

Four kids under six swaddled in wool hats mittens scarves and thick cotton duck jackets. Her husband's coat will barely close around her now the fifth child inside her. The sky is clear and huge and utterly surprising and the world seems to stretch farther than the old house the new barn and the rutted road leading down the hill to town.

At this precise moment she is happy.

Trying to claim time.

■ ☐ ☐ ☐ ☐

Dream:

The hall floor of the house changes from linoleum tile to slate. I walk very slowly and discover three rooms at the other side of the house unknown before. There are no windows on this side of the house but the air moves. I have had no knowledge of these three rooms before now. The light is a dusty golden colour and underneath the colour there is a soft and beautiful humming.

Even if their idea of claiming a space for their new home seemed only a strange dream.

It is the day before Christmas Eve. I want the something exciting to begin but it is not here yet. I am bored in my grandmother's small house.

The sun's light crackles yellow against the kitchen window. On the windowsill above the sink there is a small cracked square mirror which my grandfather uses when he shaves a jar of Noxzema a silver razor soap draining on a dish with plastic spikes shaving cream and *Joy* dish soap.
I am humming as I steady myself. Left hand on the small green door right hand gripping the frame and letting my right foot lead me slowly down the steep and narrow stairs to the basement.

— Why do you want to go down there for? There's nothing down there.

The scent of damp the scent of the ground hidden outside under the snow rose when I walked stair by stair under the house underneath the lives that were playing out upstairs.

Cigarettes being lit coffee being poured evaporated milk poured into that evaporated milk poured over cereal. It was winter and there were no flies in the kitchen. Soon cigarette smoke would look like long fingers suspended in

front of the kitchen window only a shade darker than the
morning pale grey fingers pressed against the outside glass.
The smoke would seem trapped inside wanting to get out
the cold light would seem desperate to get in through the
glass and touch our warm skin.

— Nothing down there my grandmother said.

But my small world opened underneath that house. There
was no window in the basement only a band of light from
the kitchen above shone on the rough shelves lined with
mason jars of different sizes. My grandmother had filled the
jars with colour yellow beans purple beet pickles red
raspberry jam red rhubarb jam green chow chow relish
gritty brown of Christmas pudding. Here there was colour
and quiet and the sense that I was happily surrounded by
the prospect of events past present future
sealed in rows and rows of jars. I could choose to go upstairs
and meet them or I could simply stay down here.

This was the place I most wanted to be.

My grandmother took recipes from family friends neighbours. She wrote them quickly in an orange scribbler with CANADA on the front. Interlined with margins 9 $\frac{1}{8}$" x 7 $\frac{1}{8}$" or 23.1 x 18 cm if you were so inclined.

These recipes recorded a moment of time a taste of something a piece of conversation and when she herself recreated the recipe she recreated the taste of those words and digested them again and again.

These jellies jams relishes were shared secrets. Sealed in jars and kept in the basement in neat rows.

□ □ □ □ ■

You asked for my recipe for Aunt Mary's Cookies. So here goes:
Aunt Mary's Cookies
2c sugar 4 eggs 6 tsp B Powder 2c shortening 5c flour salt
Vanilla roll & fill with Jelly.

■ □ □ □ □

It was an October day of cold rain. At lunch hour I walked to a bank machine to get out twenty bucks. I had been to this particular machine many times just behind two sets of heavy glass doors the machine encased in dark grey metal. This machine is on a wind-whipped corner 107th Street and Jasper Avenue and to make my way to it involves traversing a platform of concrete etched with the wind's own geometry the rain's trajectory arcs and triangles. It is marked as a place that needs to be found needs to be gotten to by ramps and cascading stairs. Underneath this small concrete plain the LRT station CORONA makes the spot feel to me as if I am at the very centre of things.

It is here I open the glass door to the machine insert my card and enter my PIN number. My grandmother is just behind me. I am certain of this fact and do not even think about it as I turn to talk to her. But I realize she can't be there. She has died five years before I am certain of this fact and yet I know she is there. I do not feel unsettled I do not feel frightened. I smile feeling only a sense of accomplishment because before she died she told me she would be back. And so here goes:

It has taken her longer than she intended perhaps but she has come back just the same just to let me know.

When I was in grade two I had a friend who collected birds' nests. He kept them all lined up on a shelf above the head of his bed. Each of the birds had built their own home from a memory that was already in their blood and brains when they were born. They knew how to build a place to live and maybe to die.

One nest still had an egg in it. A small exquisitely blue egg. This egg was his most treasured possession and he would never let me touch it. It was a gift that had been given to him placed in his path so that he alone would find it and I could only stand on top of his pillows and look. I was jealous that I had not been the one to see it first. If I had I would have neatly cracked the egg to look inside.

— Don't you wonder if there's anything in there?

— Sure. But it's more interesting to wonder about it than actually know.

— Well I'd rather know. There could be a dead bird in there or something. Doesn't it bother you to have something dead right over your head when you're sleeping?

— I think it probably likes having me here. I would if I were a bird. When I die I want to come back as a bird.

— When I die I want to come back as a house.

— A house? You can't come back as a house. It just sits there. It doesn't do anything.

— Okay then, I'll come back as a train and see the world.

eight

Wedding Photograph: My mother and father were beautiful on their wedding day. There wasn't a trace of the future on their faces. The two people in this photograph would very soon be gone dissolving into entirely different people. Something new.

It was a small-town marriage warranting a large photograph of the happy young couple and an accompanying newspaper article. The couple's life to be in brief outline.

The bride's white lace wedding gown featured a full-length gathered skirt and fitted lace bodice. Her white veil was held in place by a rhinestone tiara, the crowning glory. No less than 40 lace-covered buttons adorned the back of the dress. The bride declined to wear gloves instead carrying a white bible and a small bouquet of red roses with trails of white silk ribbon festooned with one red bloom each. The bride was attended by three bridesmaids.

The groom cut a handsome figure wearing a well-cut black suit, white shirt and grey-striped tie. He was attended by three groomsmen. The couple will honeymoon in Saskatoon and after which plan to permanently reside in Prince Albert.

It's just a camera trick. Camera trick.

This permanent residence was their history's starting point. A series of numbers posit the beginning of two people's lives running side by side like railroad tracks. The first station is a small house on 32nd Street West Prince Albert Saskatchewan.

There is nowhere else to go. This is home now.

■ □ □ □ □

My mother comes from a place where in winter water is just a hard crust of cold on top of the wash basin. A place where in January a narrow strip of wrist exposed to the grey light of this merciless season will ache for summer's fire.

Last seen:

— We both wanted the same things a home family and as my mother is saying this as my mother's voice is trailing off as if she too believes it to be a lie I also detect in her voice the firm turn of a wish that simply saying the words could make them true. Releasing them would transfix this wanting into some shape and now twenty years later she was hoping insisting that she could will these words into truth.

Their life together had gone off the rails off track switched to a new line.

□ □ □ □ ■

In my grade one reader was a section called HOME and on the title page was a photograph tinted surreal the round flat shadows made by her blue bike the red of the little girl's skirt the spots of pink and yellow that mark the unidentifiable flowers beside the front step. The girl is moving towards something but I know she can never get there. She is suspended in the prospect of happiness the possibility of marking a circle with the pedals of her bike. But the white door of her house is marked with TV-blue shadows and will be forever closed to her. HOME is just behind a door and she will never be able to get to it.

— *Serviceable.*

My mother used this word to describe the purpose of important wardrobe pieces. *Serviceable* was how my mother described the winter boots I wore in grade two I thought they were ugly and I hated the flat slapping sound they made when I walked on packed snow. The boots the other girls wore made a short squeak as their heels first hit the snow. They shone black and bright red against a white background.

My boots were a simple serviceable dull brown and came to mid-calf where they fastened on the side with a tab of leather and a tarnished brass buckle. I prayed for the buckle to break so I could get a new pair before I grew out of these ones.

My winter clothes were warm mismatched a navy wool coat beige fuzzy fake fur hat marbled with grey and with big pompoms tied under the chin. Thick green mittens popcorn-stitched warm. *Serviceable.*

What I wanted was a grey *muff* with a matching grey cloche hat a grey flannel winter coat and shiny black boots that went up as high as my coat. There was a girl dressed like this in a colouring book I got for Christmas and I brought to life this girl on the page as she walked through her one-dimensional world outlined in thick black lines.

It was this image of a girl I had had a hand in creating a girl I wanted to recreate in myself an image that had probably never truly existed anyway or anywhere it was simply an image of a child who was the same thickness the same plane the same dimension as the place that surrounded her it was the image of her I had in my mind when I pushed my boots to the bottom of the silver metal garbage can by the gym under paper under quarter-cut oranges and apple cores and squashed bologna sandwiches.

I walked home in my *serviceable* black oxford shoes taking the path through the school yard that was hardest packed and most slippery.

— I lost my boots Mom.

— Lost them? Where did you last see them?

— I put them by the entrance this morning and when I went to put them on after school they were gone.

— Well where did you look for them?

— All over. Maybe someone stole them.

— Did you ask at the office?

— No.

— I'll phone the school tomorrow.

— What'll I wear in the morning?

■ ◻ ◻ ◻ ◻

My mother went out to buy me a new pair of boots after my father got home after we had finished supper. She left the dishes in the sink to soak so she could get to the store before it closed.

— I want you out of the tub and in your pyjamas by the time I get home.

■ ◻ ◻ ◻ ◻

In the Army and Navy bag was a pair of high leather boots black with laces at the top. They even had a small low heel.

— I love them trying them on barefoot

— I still want you to have a look for your old ones tomorrow.

I didn't bother looking but I showed off my new boots to my friends proud to have something that beautiful. It was three days before I got up the courage to tell my mother that I had lied about my old brown boots had thrown them away not lost them. She was furious and I knew it because she said nothing.

— I can't take them back now because you've worn them. If you ever pull a stunt like this again...

I was sent to bed early and didn't say a word about it. My mother never brought it up after that night but I was happy when I finally did grow out of those black leather boots I was ashamed of their beauty ashamed of myself for wanting them in the first place.

■ ▢ ▢ ▢ ▢

A boy in a high school art class made a sketch of me in baggy jeans   red kangaroo coat and navy blue shoes with a negative heel. Underneath he had written *our shady lady*.

You can convince yourself of anything.

■ ▢ ▢ ▢ ▢

My grade ten English teacher was fresh out of university. His face was clean-shaven and he had creases ironed into his cords.

He had mug shots of the Beatles above the blackboard at the front of the class and the first few lines of "Across the Universe" written underneath their faces.

At the beginning of the year we did a little exercise on the power of words   specifically *cold pricklies* and *warm fuzzies*. Each of us had a blank sheet of paper pinned to our backs and everyone was to write a *warm fuzzy* about that person on the sheet.

When I took off the sheet someone had written *phony bitch*.

You can convince yourself of anything.

Was it then?

When my father was nineteen he contracted hepatitis and was in the hospital for three months a jaundiced skeleton in quarantine. It was then that he wrote down the only stories of his life. These were stories my mother kept for years after their marriage   stacked and tightly bound with a red elastic band. She stashed the precisely folded sheets of paper my father's nurses had ripped from notebooks and kept them in her underwear drawer

proof he had been the one to ask her to marry him.

I was thinking about when I stooked all those bales last summer. Earned enough to take us to Waskesiu. Remember? Goodtime eh??!!   Have a good time while we're young. That's what we're going to do. When I get out of this goddam hospital I'll go back to work in S'toon and you can come with me. I hope??!! I wish I would have asked you before now I hope you don't think I'm stupid. When I come home let's get married? Write me back with an answer.

Between the parallel narrow blue tracks running
horizontally on each white page were the large dark forms
of his handwriting the same writing I would remember
having seen as a child on ripped corners of envelopes or on
pages ripped out of my school scribblers numbers
determining lengths of 2 x 4s fields of plywood
estimating the cost of homes that did not yet exist. Numbers
and names and addresses written with a carpenter's pencil
he sharpened with one of my mother's good knives.

Remember when I won the $$$200 bucks playing poker? I
must have looked like one stunned bugger!! I laugh just
thinking about it. When I get some real money behind me I'm
going to buy you a fur coat a real good pair of shoes and build
us a big house. Write me back.   PS I love you.

My mother burned all his letters right after the divorce.
She was going to burn all her wedding photographs but
decided to keep just one.

There is no record of my mother writing him back. Now
there is no record of my father's stories. Only houses
apartments that came from the numbers and letters on
small lost pieces of paper.

Fear of power tools.

Drapery Study:

Bent over the chrome stacking stool in my room is a bright orange mini my mother had made from drapery fabric a fifty-cent remnant bought in Simpson-Sears' Notions department. Over the skirt is an orange nylon sleeveless shell stretched out at the bottom after three days' worth of wear.

These are my two favourite pieces of clothing and I cling to them with a superstitious fervour they are talismanic.

These two pieces of clothing become the very aspects of orange the smooth artificiality of nylon rough nubs of the skirt's tight weave.

I run my hands along the red plastic beads separating my part of the bedroom from my sister's and watch this small field of orange trap noise as my fingers impersonate picks of pink purple blue. I play these colours on strings of beads trap their light from right out of the air.

Positive becomes negative.

This photograph removes any doubt. Now I remember that I loved my father. This photograph has the opacity of a Japanese print an ancient sense of time with its pale colours a soft field of blue that is my dress tenuous marks made by the needles of the Christmas tree against the light of the flash the small smoldering dots of muted red green yellow blue. My father is smiling he must have been happy at this moment? The cross-hatched background pleated sepia curtains cold against the front window.

I know that once I loved the man in this photograph. The small Christmas tree is on top of the television and that is where I stand happy to be allowed to touch a shiny round red ornament.

My father is holding my ankles to keep me from falling. He is only twenty years old and still handsome tall and still strong in the black well-cut pleated wool trousers from his wedding suit and a shirt that is a soft grey windowpane plaid.

My father appears fascinated by me this small child he is mesmerized by my absorption in the lights my happiness and I know at this particular moment that he loved me.

This photograph proves it.

Indispensable knowledge my mother tried to give me:

> how to properly fold a towel

> how to embroider a table runner

> how to scrub a floor

— Scrub your way to a door not the other way around otherwise you'll be stuck in a corner waiting for the floor to dry.

> how to turn a collar and cuffs

I watched as she ripped out stitches   a cigarette stuck between her lips   and laid the collar and cuffs on the coffee table beside the ashtray   ganglia of threads from the severed pieces of my father's shirt. Pieces of cotton turned inside out and reattached. Frayed edges hidden closest to bare skin   a shirt looking brand new.

> how to darn socks

— You make the heel to fit over the rubber ball. It's the perfect shape and you can see what you're doing.

Wordless my mother wove yarn   in and out over and under guided by the thick silver darning needle with the huge eye.

When she finished   you could feel the shape of the hole on your heel the place where the emptiness was   *nothing* embossed on the sock and reminding you of it every time you stepped down.

■ □ □ □ □

My grandmother died in December. Our yellow Tercel whined and squealed against cold as we drove along the highway to Saskatchewan. The coffin was a fine dark burnished wood and her children and grandchildren placed a single red rose each on top. Her body was to be given to fire and when the final prayer was offered I opened my eyes. I kept my head lowered and glanced sideways at the feet of a man sitting on the metal fold-out chair in front of me. His white socks showed above the side-zipper of his black chunk-heeled platform boots. They were sorrowfully out of style but they shone with a lack of wearing. I thought of the Bee Gees. There was something solemnly absurd about the boots and I kept my head down   covering my mouth to hold in the laughter. After the funeral family and friends gathered at my grandmother's house. The windows were opaque covered with frost there was an aluminum urn full of weak coffee   a pot of Blue Ribbon brand tea.

There were two women that stuck to themselves grieved alone by the food table crowded with sandwiches cucumber relish a ham slices of cold turkey squares cookies Carnation evaporated milk opened on two sides with the tip of a sharp knife and lifted to let some air inside the tin. The two women said their goodbyes quickly nodded as they passed by the quiet group of us then quickly put on boots heavy tweed coats wrapped hand-knit scarves around their head until all we could see was their long out of fashion cat's eye glasses beginning to fog up in the cold of the back porch. The door's hinges squeaked as the women crunched their way down the steps and were gone.

— Who were they? My cousin asked. We all looked at each other in silence.

No one knew them.

Police are seeking the whereabouts:
Last seen:

I buy my oldest son a pair of gloves for Christmas. They are called *Magic Mitts* leaving fingertips exposed if necessary but allowing hands to be hidden by a small cap that can be flipped back over frozen fingers. A small square of cardboard is stapled to the two mittens and on it is printed the following caution: *Magic Mitts are for fishermen hunters roofers carpenters or trombone players.*

I have never seen a trombone player busking outside in Edmonton in winter in thirty below. I suppose that would be the magic.

■ □ □ □ □

— I only ever gamble with small change or on small things my mother said.

A little gamble was ordering surprise packages of fabric from the Sears catalogue. Something tangible and certain at the other end of a wager. The bundle was wrapped in several layers of brown paper heavy taped and tied with thick twine. Once our order contained a flowered cotton three yards of psychedelic impressions of nature in orange and

brown three yards in blue and red. My sister and I got
pantsuits variations on a theme floral studies.

— Do we look like hippies Mom? I asked when we
modeled the outfits for our father.

— Well that's the style. You both look neat and tidy
real smart.

Another gamble arrived a package of cotton with huge
blue diamonds contained in a setting of white rope
embedded in an orange background. This evolved into a vest
and matching twenty-seven-inch-wide flare-leg pants. I
wore a white beaded choker with diamonds shaped with
blue beads around my throat. I made the choker myself but
it was my mother who made the beading loom.

A wood base and two sides threaded over top like guitar
strings. The beads we strung were stored in narrow glass
vials stopped with corks. I imagined them to be the tiny
indispensable ingredients of a magic potion eye of newt
frog's tongue a baby's tears my tears.

The beads were opalescent as clouds dark as a lake
bottom. Each bead row after row was played on a fret my
mother had fashioned from three scrap pieces of 2 x 4 and
common white cotton thread. Each bead was the note of a
song she could never allow herself to sing.

A grid that breath and sound dissolve.

Childhood dreams:

— own a grey flannel pleated skirt brown penny loafers
with pennies in both shoes   white knee high socks   pink
angora sweater
— attend a finishing school in Switzerland   charm school
at the very least
— travel across Europe on the Orient Express all
by myself

■ □ □ □ □

I read my horoscope from the newspaper wearing my
pink dacron housecoat. *Love figures prominently today.* I
shared the same astrological sign as Bette Davis. I put my
palm to my forehead in a mock gesture of the vapours.
— Oh don't be so dramatic my mother said.

RECURRING FICTIONS

At the age of twenty-one I find a stage inside store windows safety behind glass to see or not be seen. When the lights inside the window are flicked off I disappear dissolving into a black felt surface absolving myself from communion beyond this glass.

Window dresser for a menswear store *haberdashery* the very word tastes of a classic fedora hat leather patches on elbows tweed. Behind glass I find a tactile pleasure repeating this word to myself a tactile pleasure in rough resistance of herringbone harris tweed caressing fine long silk ties folding soft lambswool gently stacking colours and displaying them in the store window on a shelf covered in grey flannel.

I invest the menswear patterns with their own sensuality ordered chaos of paisley on silk neat and tidy tattersall comfort of checks plaids oxford cloth solid and stripes. Inside the window I have the textures of these clothes all to myself.

Me and the bustform. Soft-coated foam form torso with hard wood neck. This is the make-believe man I poke straight pins into smoothing the front placket of shirts. I keep a neat row of pins in the cuff of my own shirt prepared and poised for the dressing of an inanimate object I animate.

Positioning the tie. Using the two bias-cut seams as my guide on the right side of the bustform's neck I make the knot four-in-hand-with-a-dimple. A beautifully consistent knot that I can achieve over and over with the elegance simplicity and permanence of a hammer striking a nail.

I feel the need to dress in the clothes I put in the windows. I buy men's clothing from the store in which I work.

I go to a barber short back and sides long on top.

— Go ahead and use the clippers I don't mind if a little skin shows oh could you please cut a little sideburn by each ear? Thanks. $4.50? Hey my kind of deal.

Haberdashery. Haver dashingly. Have a dash on me. I stuff exactly ten sheets of tissue fashioned into a cone through the sleeve of a waiting gabardine sports jacket. Gently smooth the shape of a shoulder create the contours of a man's chest inside navy gabardine.

His skin fits his bones and is no longer the colour of grey marble.

nine

Dream:

A man and woman are getting married and each has a different colour moustache. The two stand in front of a priest and there are strangers sitting in the pews behind them and everyone is serious about this. The couple is made out of paper flat and one-dimensional dolls taken out of a big book. Their clothes have already been laid out but there is no way for them to get at anything.

Still they laugh paper laughs even though their poor mouths cannot move. Oh they are laughing on the *inside*.

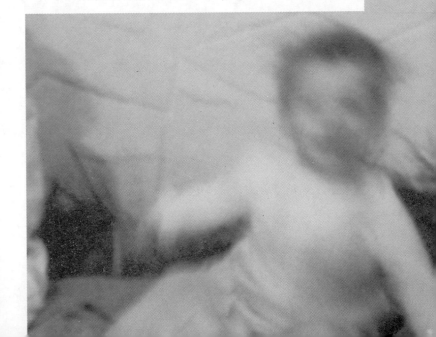

My youngest son spreads his fingers lifts my hand from underneath and moves his fingers with mine as if playing cat's cradle moving invisible strings making shapes one from another one to another geometry in thin air our hands intersecting line and shape.

He turns my hand over and points to my palm shows me before he has even learned the words the lines he sees the lines he must learn to tell the story

Past:

Present:

Future:

I carry my son to bed and as I pull the quilt over him his legs kick involuntarily.

— They're train tracks he whispers before gathering his feet under him and falling asleep.

■ □ □ □ □

Dreams of loss:

hair teeth   a child a parent.

A palm reader follows the rivers on my palm and tells me
she sees a move in my future. I will live beside water. I want
to ask her:

— Am I on the right train?

□ □ □ □ ■

December 3, 1999. No snow yet. This winter a changeling
season   winter pretends to be spring and we believe it.
Sense of suspension   the pall the cold brings is nowhere to
be found   hope that winter will never come   the season may
have been forgotten this year. Spring will follow fall? No.
Seasons make room for themselves and sadness always finds
a place.

My youngest son   his grandmother and I walk down a
hard worn path   leaning away from the edge of the Bow
River where ducks gather throughout the winter   expecting
and receiving food from strangers. I lift my son on top of a
large grey boulder   he has brought bread for the birds but
there are no ducks there to take his offering.

Ice is beginning to harden between small rocks on shore.
Winter may sneak up on us after all   the ice wanting to take

hold of the banks its fingers reaching for us. We manage to stay warm just outside its reach.

On the other side of the river train number 9543 travels past. CN Rail   a line of red cars. What is inside them all is a mystery. The three of us wave and call out across the river to the engineer. Comfort in the sound of the cars over the tracks   comfort in the whistling hum of the train's response. I gather my son close to me please do not take this moment from me.

Too much happiness cannot be trusted.

■ ☐ ☐ ☐ ☐

Coliseum Station. Morning rush hour. Standing on the concrete platform   a collage of spit blobs and cigarette butts waiting for the train downtown. With luck I should be at work in twenty minutes.

I see him sitting on the bench. I am directly in his sight. At first I can't quite believe what he is carrying   wrapped in khaki at first it doesn't register. Now there is no mistaking the shape of a small shotgun   keeping his gun warm on a cool fall morning. His t-shirt is the same color as the stiff fabric that covers his gun. A gun cozy.

He stares past me. The train is moving towards me in slow motion. The man rises. He is stout and wears gold rimmed glasses   could be somebody's grandfather.

Double bells ring the train stops the doors open I enter the same train car as this man. The doors close behind us all but the train does not move. What if he shoots? I am watching him and think I can easily crawl to the door behind me run down the stairs...

My son is in daycare and I have to be at work. I cannot move. No false moves. It is important to be quiet calm I am surprisingly calm. I breathe I think of my son what will he want for supper tonight? What books will I read to him?

— I am invincible he cannot touch me cannot hurt me. It is my own ghost speaking to me telling me this man with the gun cannot see me.

Still the train is not moving no one on the train is moving we have all turned to stone.

Two policemen. They seem to spring from a trap door where the escalator disappears back into itself. Coming towards the train they open the doors of our car and know exactly where he is.

— Stand up please.

I can barely hear them speak. I am hardly breathing. The man looks confused says nothing only rises and follows them obediently each policeman holding an arm and from behind they look as if they are helping their elderly father cross the road steadying their own flesh and blood preserving the life of someone they love. Push and pull of death.

The double bells ring once again and the train pulls away from the cool grey platform. I stare straight ahead.

At work I tell my friend there was a man with a gun on the train...

She is utterly rattled.

— Why the hell did you get on the train? Why didn't you just run?

I don't tell her that it wasn't really me on the train it was my ghost and she was telling me it would be OK whatever happened it was going to be OK.

— I really don't know I say.

My grandmother's ghost-voice inspires me to write a poem and it appears for her on city buses and trains displayed alongside ads for   chocolate bars   cell phones confidential counselling   *pregnant and confused*?

I look for the poem hold my youngest son close to my side his head against my ribs as we huddle on the seat of the train.

— Sleep if you're tired   I tell him   and his eyes close. And there is my grandmother. Right here   on the other side of me closest to the doors.

— Why the hell didn't you just get off the train?

Because nothing ever really begins   nothing ever really ends.

ten

Dream:

I am able to watch myself from above my own body. Kneeling on a large stone on an ocean shore and I must lift myself off before the water reaches me and carries me out to sea. I strain neck muscles shoulders back thighs calves my whole being is desperate to fly and yet I cannot move from this spot. I smell the salt in the water it might carry me smell the seaweed it waits for me. Slowly rising off the rock I am afraid to uncurl my legs keep them tucked under but the wind current buoys me and in one awkward jerky movement I am flying straight flying right. *Straighten up and fly right.* I am. Out over the sea but the sheet of water is like celluloid a place where my life and the life of those I remember and those I have long forgotten is played out for me by whom? *Straighten up and fly right.*

I think that song but hear another.

If I were a carpenter and you were a lady Johnny Cash
and June Carter singing about my mother and father? This is
the song that comes to my mind. Do ghosts have a mind?
Can ghosts think? And yet I hear this song a guitar and a
harmonica. Unlikely instruments for astral travel. Is this
what it is not a dream of flying the ghost of my past
life/past lives the ghost of the lives of anyone I have ever
known? People passing in cars going the opposite direction
people waiting at bus stops people framed by windows in
office towers anonymous faces. Anon.

I am naked flying naked invisible to the naked eye but
it's not really flying my body is simply suspended by some
force an invisible force and I take it quite for granted.

There is my father.

There is my father unafraid. Unafraid of power saws or
huge trucks full of cement or planes of smooth wood
carried as if they were sheets of vellum knots in the
plywood like watermarks. The smell of sawdust is my
father's skin. Deep brown skin on his arms ending
at his elbows where the lines of his shirt sleeves begin lines
drawn with sun's pigment beating down on him as he
worked outside.

Last seen:

I have awakened to a quiet house. Something is wrong.
My mother is sleeping my sister and brother are in
their beds.

I shake my mother's shoulder.

— Where's Dad?

— Work she answers with her eyes closed.

— I didn't say good-bye to him I didn't say goodbye why
didn't you wake me up so I could say goodbye?

I cry until she shouts at me STOP gives up and covers
her head with the bedspread I cry until my sister and

brother are both awake. I jump up and down and I cry until my voice is hoarse and I have a headache and I can feel the eyes in my head and my mouth is dry and my heels hurt from hitting the floor.

— Phone him! Where is he? When will he be home? Just phone him!

I don't know where he is working or how to find the job site or if I would even be able to make it all the way there.

— When will he be home? I didn't get a chance to say goodbye!

■ ☐ ☐ ☐ ☐

— Just after we got engaged your dad came over to see me and asked me to make him a sandwich I said we had nothing in the house except dog food so he'd have to eat what I made him. He thought I was joking.

She laughed and looked over at my father who was staring at the table brushing away an imaginary crumb. Poured herself a cup of tea holding the handle of the pot with her right hand while cradling the spout and holding a cigarette with her left hand.

— Well I was laughing so hard as I made it I could hardly stand up tears in my eyes I was laughing so hard. I set it on the table. You asked me if it was dog food it sure smelled like dog food and I said now do you really think I would make you eat a dog food sandwich? Of course it was and he ate the whole thing too polite to say anything.

She took a drag from her cigarette and started to laugh softly at first little puffs of smoke escaping from her nostrils and mouth and then she laughed so hard that smoke came out in one big cloud like the smoke from an old-fashioned train speeding out of control along the track.

Either my father did not hear or only pretended not to he smoked his cigarette flicked the ashes into the cuff of his work pants.

I couldn't swallow maybe it was the thought of choking down dog food maybe it was just plain fear. In that moment I realized my parents had suddenly turned into different people. These were not the mother and father I knew.

Where had the real ones gone?

— See? My mother said looking over at me. We didn't have all the things you kids do now and we still had fun.

Last seen:

I am ten years old and it is our family's first holiday. We drive to Banff.

On the outskirts of Calgary I see the mountains. At first I think they are clouds or the huge teeth of some gigantic beast that is hiding just under the surface of the earth. I keep looking for them making sure they are not going anywhere.

Now we are through Calgary and I can see the mountains clearly.

— I never liked the mountains my mother says. They make me feel all hemmed in like they're right on top of you. She tells us of the six weeks she spent here before she and my father were married and the guy who fell in love with her and how she had given him the brush off and come back to Saskatchewan to get married. I think she has had an exciting life and hope I'll get the chance to give boys the brush off when I get older. But I think that if I had had the chance to live in Banff I would have taken it.

— Why didn't you come and live here with Mom? I ask my father.

— What would I have done? he says and I have no answer. I don't know what he did before he married my mother. He has never said.

We take a gondola to the top of Sulphur Mountain. Before we get on my mother takes a picture of my father my sister my brother and me. My father is well dressed with a brown cardigan over a blue shirt his hair is neat and combed back with Brylcreem.

His hands are big and thick-fingered his wedding band cuts into his ring finger. His left hand rests on my shoulder the right on my brother's my sister stands smiling between us. My father is only faintly smiling or perhaps he is only squinting against the sun he seems to be gathering us in. At that moment I remember him happy. Now I am not so sure.

We are so small standing in front of him.

A mimeographed copy of the outdoor rink skating schedule taped to the inside of the cereal cupboard door. I wait all week for Friday Night Public Skate.

As I round the corner from our house I can see the rink in the schoolyard. It has the magic of a world wonder small crystals of ice in the air caught in light from the big floods over the ice. The night glows.

I can barely see over the boards. I wear a thick navy-blue cable-knit sweater of my father's. My mother has accidentally shrunk it and the ribbing stops at my knees it is warm and wearing it makes me think of my father.

I practise cross-overs skating backwards figure **8s** my skates making marks in the ice indentations in a substance that will disappear in just a few weeks the lines I am making will no longer be visible but the imprint will linger somewhere perhaps in this light-charged air perhaps in the ice itself melting into the packed grass underneath my skates.

Tunes from a top-forty station blare from the tinny speakers. Teenagers boyfriends and girlfriends skate together holding hands.

I skate until I can no longer feel my toes. Hobble into the skating shack its floor ripped and chewed by the picks and blades of skates smell of the small gas stove in the corner

wet wool. I unlace my skates and the pain in my toes almost

makes me cry. I shove my feet into my boots tie my skate

laces together and run home. My feet burn from the cold.

It is only when I am inside the back door of our house

that I start crying. My father runs to me picks me up

quickly takes off my boots and socks and rubs my toes

between his hands as fast as he can. He makes a funny face

and the pain of heat and blood coming back into my toes is

so intense his face screwed up so tight I begin to laugh.

— Move them around he tells me wiggle them back
and forth.

I bend them forward and backward. He has saved me. My

father has saved me. I love this man.

— There. You're all fixed up now he says.

In that second I cannot imagine him gone.

□ □ □ □ ■

My sister and I are listening to eight-tracks in my

basement bedroom beige walls brown shag carpet and a

black light poster Work Hard and You Will Be Rewarded

the cartoon character has a knife in his back. There is one

small rectangular window and the room is cool even in the

August heat. I sit cross-legged at the base of a full-length mirror and put on make up blue eye shadow navy blue mascara use a hot curling iron to flip my hair away from my face I am getting ready to drive three miles over to my boyfriend's house. Convinced I am in love I still can not imagine that he will hurt me and a few years later I will consider sending him a thank you card for doing so and saving my life. Right now though it seems that I love this boy more when I am not with him.

This boy plays hockey and I imagine that I will travel from NHL team city to NHL team city with him.

My father has insulted this boy.

— He skates knock-kneed.

I am in love and indignant. But this boy stops phoning me suddenly and when I telephone a couple of weeks later his mother says he's not home.

It is this particular night that my father comes down to my room to talk to my sister and me.

— Time for bed he says. My parents have a couple over for drinks and we hear their laughter upstairs.

My dream of being the hockey wife building and re-building a life in city after city watching my well-built hockey husband sit on the bench spit in the penalty box take a stick to the head throw down his gloves chase a frozen puck back and forth across the ice has vanished. Now I am a seventeen-year-old wondering what will I do with the rest of my life? Had I noticed the similarity between NHL and NIHILISM?

    — Why did you marry Mom? I ask my father.

    — Because I thought I was in love he says and laughs.

□ □ □ □ ■

There were boxes of nails in the back of my father's red work truck. Nails of various shapes sizes some small as pins with hardly any head at all some like railroad spikes dark with an oily sheen. My father hammered these nails into pieces of wood hammering their heads again and again and again. This is the image I so wanted to see when you ordered a Rusty Nail. These rusty nails you got hammered on whiskey in a glass rot gut rust gut you watched rusted-out strippers squeaky-boned love a fireman's pole prop centre stage.

    — I wanted you to see what happens to some women.

Me not yet one.

— I wanted you to see what can happen   I just wanted you to see. You don't need to tell your mother I took you here. Okay?

We are sitting at a table close to the wall but your face is unrecognizable. You are a stranger   a stranger who said nothing to no one only shifting your gaze from glass of straight rye to the woman on stage   automatically taking off pieces of clothing   pivoting on stilettos.

The colour of her skin changed chameleon-like in perfect time to the spotlights   red   yellow   blue   green. She was camouflaged   hidden even though naked   moving oblivious to the few men whose faces were like my father's   lone men in dingy light expressionless as the tinny music blasted.

What was different between me and the woman on the stage? We both had breasts   sinew bone muscle and skin. Why did I feel ashamed?

My father ordered a rye and water this time and a plate of dry spareribs. I simply wanted to be invisible. Wanted that vacancy to spread outward from my heart and burn my flesh into nothing   my bones into nothing   me into nothing   but a ghost   a shade opening white onto the shadows created by the television's glow on the living room wall in winter at five o'clock before my mother caught up to the sudden dark and would turn on the overhead light   a shade touching the red bow on the birthday present that turned out to be the doll I wanted   her skin smelling of plastic   sweet and new

the doll still had all her hair and all her fingers and toes a

shade sitting beside my mother on the train to visit my aunt

my mother's belly round with my sister still asleep and

oblivious inside her   what is it my mother is thinking as she

sits staring out the train window her shoulders moving

almost imperceptibly in time to the movement of the train

I can almost decipher her thoughts   they come to me in a

shape that is like music and unlike anything I have ever

understood before to be true. Here on the train sitting

invisible beside my mother   I look to the seat across from

her and see myself.

   I know I am going home.

FLOWER

BENOIT home FLOWER FLOWER

FLOWER WORD flower

WORD

WORD

house house house house house

Last seen:

He lay for four days in the hallway of the emergency ward
still wearing the red denim pants he wore his last day of
work. Frayed at the hems of both legs the dirt ground into
them he refuses to take them off.

Last seen:

Room in the emergency ward Royal Alexandra Hospital
Edmonton. I watch my sister and I approach his bed the
energy sifts out our bodies sand draining from an
hourglass. It is late afternoon that much I know. This is my
father that much I know but he has metamorphosed. In the
past twenty years I have hardly seen him hardly heard his
voice. He is afraid.

His own father has carried him into the hospital.

Last seen:

A framing of bones top teeth and bottom teeth missing sparse white hair skin ashen like the thin blanket covering him like the hospital gown snapped shut over his right shoulder.

Last seen:

A puppet suspended by hollow strings of intravenous tubing. Liquids draining into his veins.

His chest so full of fluid it obscures his lungs a grey cloud. On the right side of his chest an incision is made to drain the fluid that has descended. Cloud busting.

Afterwards unconscious in ICU his body spasms expelling the last of the fluid from the bottom of his lungs.

Positive becomes negative.

■ ☐ ☐ ☐ ☐

Two different lines running parallel on the same track. Part of the same story. The trick is to find an ending. The trick is to find a beginning. The trick is to define precisely the points where the two lines join or come apart or join again.

Maybe they never come apart. Maybe they were never joined in the first place.

■ ☐ ☐ ☐ ☐

There were weeks when there was a puzzling suspicious silence between my mother and father. I realized very early that there was an edge a sharpness that existed between them. Those periods of

— Yep

— Nope answers to

— We outta sugar?

— Anything good on the idiot box tonight?

seemed to dissolve after a time. There would not be a lot of conversations no laughter between them but their silence seemed no longer a threat.

My mother remembers:

— You screamed and cried for two hours. Remember that time because you didn't wake up in time to give him a kiss before he left for work?

— I was afraid he would die. I was afraid I wouldn't see him again.

□ □ □ □ ■

Photograph: Eight months pregnant with my brother and my mother stops to smile while I take a picture   she is rolling the dirt in the front yard smooth with a metal roller so heavy I cannot even budge it. I can barely lift the handle.

Smoothing the crust of her corner pie-shaped lot so she can scatter grass seed and plant trees.

Is this the beginning of my parents' story? This must be the place where it all begins to unfold or   unravel.

eleven

Every spring we were dewormed. My mother assumed as her mother had before her and probably her mother before her that all children came through the other side of winter with wriggly parasites of some form invaders of stomach and intestines.

My mother mixed an orangey powder in a glass of water and stirred it until she created a little whirlpool of pale apricot.

Diffuse light the tailings of winter shone through the blinds on the kitchen window and cast stripes like fingers already closing around the glass.

— Drink it quick my mother said

I clutched the glass and looked at the still swirling liquid. Drank it down in five gulps exactly and fought to keep the whole thing from coming back up.

Every spring we were forced to swallow cod liver oil. My mother was convinced that every child came through the other side of winter with some deficiency   a lack

of vitamins
of sunlight
of fresh air.

— You look like hothouse plants she would say to us.

Pale from winter we would sit over the heat register and clutch our knees our pants tucked into our socks.

Bodies added to and subtracted from the seasons.

■ □ □ □ □

The oldest human footprint is discovered in Chauvet cave a place in which I have never walked.

It is the small light impression of an unknown unnamed ten-year-old boy left behind on the cave floor undisturbed for thirty thousand years. The silence of this step is the beginning of a story the beginning of connected sounds inside the cave's mouth.

Where did this story or any other begin? Why choose this one and not another? Beginning in the throat on the tongue? Or does this evolution begin with a place? Something beneath our feet? Let's start with *earth* or *home.* We can always make up more as we go along. When will we ever learn?

□   □   □   □   ■

Collecting. Hoarding. A dark closet full of shoes black oxfords mules mary janes doc martens velvet chunk-heeled loafers sandals flip-flops. A closet floor obliterated with shoes smelling of leather.

□   □   □   □   ■

This pine drawer is veneration to paisley. Vintage scarves in paisley. It is a link to what? I have not yet ascertained pattern a life form an amoeba moving matter. A fine silk can fix it forty-year-old synthetic fabric can hold it fast.

I impose order on my thoughts   unfold and refold these scarves   each one smooth and rich and describing every colour and movement painted by the word *experience*. The yellow ochre stretch of hands coiling outward in the morning   red laughter drinking martinis in Calgary in a restaurant with cement walls   the turquoise blue of cool sand fingers reaching down to touch the clay underneath.

I wear a chartreuse and pink paisley scarf in the last picture taken of my grandmother and me. In the photograph my hair is wild and I look as if I have been crying. The scarf is diaphanous   it sympathetically lets through light   and scent of skin. But it is also deceptively strong   printed with black fibril roots   fingers   of a pattern that creates strength by its very own movement   gathering momentum   gathering in the heartbeat   the pulse of blood felt right at the throat.

I hold this scarf to my face   it becomes a photograph of my grandmother and me. In this pattern is the story of all the words we ever said to each other.

— I don't want you to die

— We all get a second chance. I'll come and tap you on the shoulder   how about on New Year's Eve? She laughed and touched my cheek.

— How can you be so sure? What if we don't?

— I guess I'll soon find out.

On my grandmother's dresser were three plastic red
roses in a white plastic vase. The vessel was shaped like a
Greek vase amphora with a raised pattern of vertical lines
embossed around the outside. The pattern remained the
same perfect and infinite replaying the same scenes over
and over again.

☐ ☐ ☐ ☐ ■

Her letters always closed crowded in the bottom right
hand corner on a piece of paper she had torn out of
somewhere found someplace trying to squeeze in a few
more words squeeze in some time put a pen to paper
quickly tell a story. She could never seem to get the ending
quite right.

She was always hoping for something to change.

I've got your Grampa on a pretty short tether these days
there's enough to be done around here brush to burn and the
fence around the pig pen is almost fallen over. If I keep him

busy he can't get into too much trouble. Ha! Ha! Better close
for now.

Love Gramma.

And for a couple of weeks she could keep him busy   he
would even come into the house following a regular pattern
of time   for coffee and meals.

— You don't know how to make a decent stew woman
my grandfather said to her stirring a huge dutch oven full of
chunks of beef onion parsnip celery carrot potato. The
blood from the meat turning to foaming bubbles on top of
the broth.

— Godammit just get out of my way so I can cook the
thing. I've been cooking my whole life...

— You don't know what you're talking about.

— I sureashell do now get out of my way. You're sober for
a few days and you suddenly wake up to what you're eating?

— You can't do anything right. You never could and you
never will.

— Fine. Here go ahead   you do it then. Go ahead and eat
the whole pot. I hope you choke on it.

My grandmother's two poodles were barking now
jumping up on her their claws making small fast clicking
noises on the old linoleum floor. She patted her trouser
pockets for cigarettes took out her Sweet Caps and pulled
one out tapping it on the flat table she made of the package

resting in her hand. She walked to the living room the dogs following in their jumpy nervous way too angry to say anything but thinking he might be right about her after all. She'd never admit it to him never give him the satisfaction of admission.

She turned on TV folded her legs up on the chesterfield and watched noon hour Kinsmen Bingo she might have a card here somewhere. The furnace coughed on she took a drag from her cigarette. A small white ball was spit out of the drum. B–4. That was funny. She couldn't remember what it was like before this.

□ □ □ □ ■

Thanksgiving:

My sister and her boyfriend my brother me and my boyfriend. My mother had made turkey mashed potatoes cabbage rolls perogies cream puffs and pumpkin pie. A cigarette dangled from my sister's mouth as she set a bowl of turnips on the table. Her hair was still a bit damp from her shower.

We all sat in. My mother had put a quilt under the red plastic table cloth so the hot bowls of food wouldn't mark the wood underneath.

There was an empty chair at the table where my father should have been sitting. Instead he sat by himself on a metal folding chair in the garage. Smoking a cigarette finishing off a beer from the dozen in front of him staring out the open garage door. He was dressed in a plaid shirt and vest it was already cold and smelling of winter.

— Go tell your Dad supper's on the table my mother said to my sister.

— I already did. He said he's not coming in. Guess he'd rather just sit there and drink.

— Well he's not hurting anyone but himself.

— That's what he said.

After we had finished and the food had gone cold we left the table. He came inside then washed his hands and face and sat down at the table by himself.

We watched television in the living room. Red shag carpet underfoot.

He ate in silence the click of his knife and fork cold against the plate cold against the food. There was a scraping sound as his fork cleaned his knife of sour cream or tomato from the cabbage rolls or small bits of mashed potato that clung to the metal. What he was eating must have been ice cold but he had two plates full.

When he was finished he made the shape of an **X** on his plate with his knife and fork lit a cigarette from the half-finished pack of Export As in his shirt pocket. We heard the door to the garage bang shut as he went back outside.

Last seen:

X   marks the spot.

□   □   □   □   ■

— The spot on my lung has stopped growing he tells me. That's what the doctor said anyway. But I know it has not stopped. The cancer is merely resting waiting.

— Enjoy this time the doctor has said you're going to crash and when you crash you're going to crash hard.
My father denies this.
— I've been self-medicating for the past few years he tells the doctor.
— Oh yeah? The doctor smiles pulls down the thick grey wool sock to check my father's grey and swollen left foot.
— With tobacco and rye. You know?

My father's hair has begun to fall out. The strands cling to the white pillow behind him like the fine lines of an etching. I look for a story to present itself arrange itself on the pillow letters words complete sentences perhaps the truth about what he has done with his life for the past twenty years. I also look for a lie a recurring fiction.

■ □ □ □ □

He is too weak to care for himself has trouble walking leans on a cane skin hanging from his bones. He moves from the cancer ward to a nursing home.

We are told he probably will not make it to Christmas. I wait for some acknowledgment of the life he has lived this past twenty years some recognition. There is none. For him it seems as if the past twenty years have not happened. Nothing has changed. He has not let his life unravel has not lived in the dead of booze. Does booze have a half-life?

Maybe he has only been half-alive. Maybe he has been living a life but it is running alongside ours joined invisibly but never actually meeting until twenty years of running have passed and we all crash into each other.

The nursing home smells of feet and piss and rising bread dough and some unidentified something being served for

the residents to eat. Each room is a coffin. Each patient is
waiting to go somewhere else.

There is nowhere else to go. Is this home now?

□ □ □ □ ■

My father actually begins to look better. His skin fits his
bones and is no longer the colour of grey marble. Not
smoking. Not drinking.

He leans on a cane when he walks. Out the glass door
opaque from condensation past the plant pots not yet
emptied of last fall's sunflowers petunias marigolds? A
blast of cold air and he descends the concrete steps to the
parking lot holding tightly to the wrought iron railing. His
baseball cap sits high on top of his head and he wears his
faded frayed red jeans.

The food in the nursing home is unbearable to him. He
complains.

— They use instant coffee here. I can't drink the water in
this place tap water it'll kill me.

He leaves the nursing home to eat whenever he can.
McDonald's the food fair at the mall the gas station down
the road. Pop a chocolate bar and today's paper.

The other people there are unbearable to him. Just one
floor below is a ward for alcoholics.

— They drink down there you know. They walk around with a jug right in the open.

I can only look at him hunched on his unmade bed food spilled on his clothes his hair still not grown back and think: As opposed to you? Who managed to hide your drinking from us for a long time before we finally realized. As opposed to you? Who thought himself so good at hiding things or thinking you were hiding things. And for a long time you did. Building walls closing doors on yourself seems to have been your specialty.

I pity him.

I hate him.

Fortieth birthday. The day is cold not smelling of spring. The day has the scent of winter like a season has changed its mind and gone back underground. I am calm and happy this day. I have people I love.

— Don't look outside my husband tells me. There's about eight inches of snow on the ground.

Even before I pull aside the curtain I can feel the cold through the window.

— Forty years old snow on the ground in April.

— When it snows I get the feeling that there is a white roof over my head. It's a good feeling my son says.

□ □ □ □ ■

April 13: Today it is minus twenty with the wind chill. It is winter without snow. A season cheating on us. A season trying to fool us all into believing it is something it's not.

Phony bitch.

— We'll meet you at McDonald's I tell my father. My son and I drive past the basement suite where his grandfather is now living. A room in a large brick house on a quiet street across from a school yard.

We see him sitting outside the house in his truck. A red Ford pick-up he was driving twenty years ago. The same truck I used to watch for when I walked down streets not knowing where he was alive or dead. The same truck I used to look for parked outside the homes I have lived over the past two decades. Now here it is. Scratched and rusty with a mismatched white door.

■ ◻ ◻ ◻ ◻

— I'm going in for cigarettes my father shouted his hand already turning the knob to the garage door the dog barking out of habit more than anything it was too small to do anything but offer a warning even if a stranger were trying to come into the house.

— Wait I'm coming and I would be ready to go to town in minutes seconds glad to escape from our house on the acreage feeling I was so far from everything everywhere I wanted to be everywhere else.

The truck radio usually blared straight top forty but after eight o'clock the announcer played album cuts from Pink Floyd Mott the Hoople Supertramp. When the truck reached the top of the hill going into town and the sunset was a sad end of summer yellow orange red I really felt as if I had a place to go to. I just hadn't found it yet.

There was a Cuban Lunch on the truck's dashboard that had melted in the sun and hardened again into another shape entirely. The peanuts in chocolate were still identifiable.

Police are seeking the whereabouts:

My father held a lit cigarette in his hand squinting against the sun setting over the crest of the freshly tarred road. We could hear the tar small hard spurts against the side of the truck as the wheels shot the goo.

— When can I start smoking in the house? I asked him

— When you can buy your own cigarettes.

— Will you buy me some gum then?

— Yep.

My youngest son and I meet my father at McDonald's. This time he waits for us in the parking lot salutes us with his coffee waving the paper cup slowly back and forth to us when we drive in. Park between the white lines that show us where to stop where to start.

The wind is blowing so strongly it is difficult for me to open the car door and it slams behind me as I walk to the passenger side to open the door for my son take him out of his seat.

— I'll meet you inside my father says. He squints against the wind pulls his coat collar up around his neck retreats into the coat's warmth. We follow him into the restaurant bending our heads down against the wind. My hands are already cold.

Ahead of me in line my father orders another coffee.

— I'll get that Dad I say.

— Didn't anyone tell you I'm a big boy now? I can pay for my own stuff. Smiles.

— Well I'm paying for our food anyway.

He shakes his head. His skin is greyish and there are dark circles under his eyes.

— It's OK.

Last seen:

— Aren't you ordering any breakfast?

— No I gotta lose some weight. See? And he smoothes the front of his plaid flannel shirt over his belly. Gettin' fat.

With a trust that has yet to be challenged my four-year-old son walks beside his grandfather into the play area while I wait for our food. He looks back at me and I smile at him meaning it's all right to go in without me.

My boy has already disappeared into a blue plastic tube when I place the tray on the table beside my father.

— I'm here I shout into the air to let my son know where I am.

— I'm here Mom and I see his small face grinning back through a Plexiglas window above me.

My father slaps a copy of the *Bargain Finder* on the table.

— What are you looking for?

— If there's a bargain I'll find it he laughs. I'm thinking of getting a couple fan-tail pigeons.

— Better ask your landlord Dad.

— Their tails are so heavy it's hard for them to fly. You wouldn't want to leave them alone cats hawks they just grab them and feast on them. You have to be on your toes all the time if you have pigeons. *While they're in the beer parlour having a union meeting other business was being developed* ... he laughs at this.

Last seen:

— When did you have pigeons Dad?

— Oh when I was young. I had all different kinds. I wanted to have some rabbits too. Had a cousin who had rabbits but we didn't have a very big farm eh? Dogs used to go by his rabbits and bark at them through the wire and the rabbit's back legs would just freeze. They'd just freeze and die.

My father phones me in the middle of the day. It is a
Wednesday in May.

— I've been to a buncha garage sales. Bought a painting. A
real one. On canvas.

— That's good. What did you pay for it?

— Lots.

— Well if you like it then it's worth it Dad.

— The woman had two but I liked the colours in this one
a bit better so I took it. You'll have to come and see it some
time.

— I will.

Offhandedly he says

The doctor thinks I probably won't make it past the
summer.

□ □ □ □ ■

Black velvet painting above the brown chesterfield. The
mountains are triangles articulated in white with green pine
trees behind the log cabin. Smoke swirls perpetually out of
the field stone chimney. A river flows in front of the cabin in
pale blue waves. I kneel on the cushion and run my finger
slowly over the hard paint there are spaces between the

colours that are soft black fur close cropped. My fingers
rest lightly on the sky a sunset feeling of pink purple
orange.

The nap of velvet is the shadow out of which the people
in my family will emerge if I stare at the painting long
enough. I am certain we are all in there somewhere me my
sister my brother my mother my father. We are all in the
black velvet painting alternately hard and soft all with the
possibility of a place a new place a new house a new
home where there would be no strange silence between
my parents.

I look at the two of them sitting after supper at the
kitchen table a fake brown woodgrain arborite edged with
silver chrome. My father blows smoke from his mouth his
lips shaped the same way as someone playing the flute. My
mother inhales her cigarette her cheeks becoming hollow
before a white cloud escapes all at once from her mouth. She
seems to be pretending there is no one else in the room.
My father brushes imaginary crumbs from beside his
empty plate.

The smoke from my parents' cigarettes floats noiselessly
above their heads suspended for a split second on the
stippled ceiling and then disappears to the four corners of
the canvas above them.

Acknowledgements

Thanks to my husband John for his encouragement and understanding, and to Eamon and "B" who make every day a joyous event. (Thanks to Brendan for the drawing on page 133.)

Cheers to my friends and family—to Shelly Hines for suggesting the "practical thing," and Linda Gauthier, Shelagh Kubish and Elaine Hoogewoonink for their initial responses to the work.

Thanks to my mother, Ann Burgos, for her strength, her determination—and for the images used in this book.

Thanks to my father for giving me the tools I needed after all.

I extend thanks to CBC Radio for producing and broadcasting a part of this novel as "Harmonicas: The Sound of Trains." Thanks also to *Prairie Fire* for publishing a portion of this novel in Volume 21, number 2 (Summer 2000) as third-prize winner in the publication's 1999 Short Fiction Contest.

A portion of this novel took shape in a University of Alberta creative writing class in which I was enrolled several years ago. Thanks to Kristjana Gunnars and my fellow students for their input.

Finally, thanks to Leslie Vermeer, my editor at the University of Alberta Press, who believed in the beauty of this book, and to Alan Brownoff for his sensitivity to the work.

I would also like to acknowledge a number of sources which provided inspiration for this novel:

Dr. Jean Clottes, "30,000 Years Before Van Gogh—the Rock Art of the Chauvet Cave," lecture at the Provincial Museum of Alberta, Time Travellers series, Edmonton, 25 March 2000.

Nat King Cole, "Straighten Up and Fly Right," 1943.

Tim Hardin, "If I Were a Carpenter," 1966.

Norman MacLaren, director, *Pas de Deux* (National Film Board of Canada, 1968).

Paul McKee, M. Lucile Harrison, Annie McCowen, Elizabeth Lehr, editors, *Jack and Janet* (Thomas Nelson & Sons [Canada] Ltd. Toronto, 1958).

Andy Ogle, "Masters of a Mammoth Riddle," *Edmonton Journal,* 25 March 2000, B4.

E.T. Rouse, "Orange Blossom Special," 1939.

Geoff Stephens, "Winchester Cathedral," 1966.

Ian Tyson, "Four Strong Winds," 1963.